Praise for Bonnie Dee's
The Countess Takes a Lover

"By the end of this deliciously enthralling tale, I was left wanting a Chris of my own. The Countess Takes a Lover is a sexy historical romance I Joyfully Recommend!"

~ *Shayna, Joyfully Reviewed*

"Ooh, now this is a story to stoke your inner cougar ...The role-reversal does some most amusing wonders for this story, I must say, because I find myself tickled at times as to how these characters can play so beautifully into the roles normally reserved for the opposite sex."

~ *Mrs. Giggles*

"Their sexual escapades seem filled with mutual emotion as the lessons progress. And some of these lessons are imaginative and lend piquancy to their time together."

~ *Aggie Tsirikas, Just Erotic Romance Reviews*

"It was truly refreshing to see a mature female character in that of Meredith. She makes no excuses about her reputation or her lifestyle. She is a woman of the world, but when it comes to Christopher, all the walls she has built up tumble down..."

~ *Karen Garrabrant, Romance Reviews Today*

"A welcome change from the usual run of romantic stories is that the hero is both the socially awkward and the inexperienced one in the relationship. ...one of the things that attracts Meredith to Christopher is the fact that behind his bookishness hides a strong and passionate personality."

~ *Azteclady, Karen Scott's Blog*

"Dee pulls off an entertaining role reversal here. Meredith is the jaded, sexually experienced one. Christopher is the dreamy virgin. He never seems weak or wimpy though. It's that whole brain as the sexiest organ idea..."

~ *Devon, The Good, the Bad and the Unread*

"Bonnie Dee has penned a delightful and very thoughtful novel with THE COUNTESS TAKES A LOVER. I found it utterly enchanting and quickly became overwhelmed at the emotions it invoked in me."

~ *Natasha Smith, Romance Junkies*

Look for these titles by
Bonnie Dee

Now Available:

Evolving Man
Opposites Attract
Blackberry Pie
Perfecting Amanda
The Valentine Effect
The Final Act
The Countess Lends a Hand
Finding Home (with Lauren Baker)

A Gifted Story
Empath

Print Anthologies
Midsummer Night's Steam: Heat Wave
Strangers in the Night

Coming Soon:

The Thief and the Desert Flower
Butterfly Unpinned (with Laura Bacchi)

The Countess Takes a Lover

Bonnie Dee

A SAMHAIN PUBLISHING, LTD. publication.

Samhain Publishing, Ltd.
577 Mulberry Street, Suite 1520
Macon, GA 31201
www.samhainpublishing.com

The Countess Takes A Lover
Copyright © 2009 by Bonnie Dee
Print ISBN: 978-1-60504-158-2
Digital ISBN: 1-59998-937-9

Editing by Linda Ingmanson
Cover by Anne Cain

First Samhain Publishing, Ltd. electronic publication: May 2008
First Samhain Publishing, Ltd. print publication: March 2009

Dedication

Thanks to all my loyal readers for sharing my journey with me.

Chapter One

"Quite simply, Madame la Comtesse, my son is a booby." Lord Richard Whitby sat on the velvet cushion of the fragile gilt seat. The chair was far too small for such a large man and his knees rose awkwardly before him.

In the elegantly appointed salon, he looked as out of place as a bear that had wandered into a millinery shop. The image of the walrus-mustached man trying on hats decorated with ostrich plumes and flowers amused Meredith. She hid her smile by sipping from the bone china teacup in her hand.

Placing the cup back on the saucer and setting it aside, she prompted him. "Pray of what concern is this to me, sir?" She laced her fingers together on her blue satin-draped lap and arched a quizzical eyebrow.

"I've heard... That is, I've been given to understand that on occasion you've taken a young man...under your wing, as it were." His face reddened and he shifted on his chair, boot heels digging into her floral carpet.

"Under my wing?" Of course, she understood, but chose to watch him squirm and flounder for words—a small amusement to brighten a dreary day.

"You'll take a young gentleman in hand and educate him in...accomplishments that might further his understanding of the fairer sex."

"Take him as a lover, do you mean?" she asked just to see his face grow even more florid.

The gentleman rose from the chair and walked toward the fireplace, a hand tapping nervously against his leg. Perhaps he found it easier to pose his proposition when not looking into her eyes.

"Yes, madame." Whitby fingered the carved ivory tusk resting on the mantle. It was an odd choice for a lady's salon, but she kept it there to remind herself of her late husband, who'd brought it back from one of his trips to the Dark Continent.

"Let me be frank. As I said, my son is a booby, a nincompoop, a weak-kneed nancy. I don't believe I shall ever see any progeny at the rate he's going. I wish him to become a red-blooded man. In short, I want him to grow up."

"Perhaps this is something you should discuss with your son." She traced her finger around the rim of her cup, enjoying the sensation of the delicate china against her fingertip.

The man heaved a sigh and turned away from the fireplace. "That is impossible. Talking to him is like finding one's way through a fog bank. His head is..." He spread his hands. "Not in the world we inhabit I can assure you. Unfortunately, he has an academic's mind and would be perfectly happy spending the rest of his life at university or playing with his posies rather than behaving like a proper man."

"I see." She knew the type—a man so enamored of knowledge that he had no room in his head for earthly pleasures.

Walking back to the little chair, Whitby perched on the edge once more. "When my son was younger, I overlooked his propensity toward bookishness, thinking he would abandon it once women caught his attention. That hasn't happened."

"How old is the lad?" Her curiosity was piqued despite her full intention of shooting down Whitby's ridiculous proposal.

"Hardly a lad anymore." He heaved a sigh. "Twenty-five. Finished at Cambridge yet still laboring at cataloging and studying his infernal plants!" He clicked his tongue and shook his head.

"You want him to take an active interest in your business concerns."

"I don't give a damn about that. I have men of affairs to run the estate. What I want is a son who'll cut a swath in society, gamble, drink and ride to hounds like any normal gentleman, a son who'll find an appropriate wife and get her with child."

The countess laughed. "You believe I can help you with all that, sir?"

"I believe you are capable of turning a boy into a man. When sensual desires are awakened, the rest of those things will naturally follow."

"Why not take him to a bordello? That is a common rite of passage, is it not?"

"When Christopher was nineteen, I attempted that. He wouldn't, er, take the bait, as it were. Too high-minded to indulge in a bit of fluff. In all honesty, I don't believe the boy's ever..." He raised his eyebrows significantly. "But a woman like you could take him in hand without ever letting him know he was being handled. You could teach him the things he needs to know not just in the bedchamber but in the ballroom. You could make a real man of him."

"Please, sir, I assure you tales of my prowess have been exaggerated. Besides, why would I be interested in such an endeavor?"

The red flush was back in full force. "I suppose 'for the challenge' would not be sufficient recommendation and so I've come up with a monetary proposal to tempt you." He cleared his throat and produced a folded sheet of paper from his breast pocket, which he handed to her.

The countess took it in one gloved hand and glanced at the number. "A generous figure." She looked at the man fidgeting before her. "You do realize, sir, that I am not a whore?"

His face became scarlet. "Of course not! I didn't mean to offend, but I was given to understand—"

"However," she continued, folding the paper carefully along the crease and offering it back to him. "I'm not averse to accepting favors in return for favors, between friends. For instance, if I were to ask you in your capacity as a member of Parliament to rally support on behalf of a particular bill, I would expect your cooperation."

"Oh." He blinked, and then a smile shone across his florid countenance at the realization he would lose nothing financially and could still accomplish his goal. "That would be entirely possible. Quite possible indeed, provided you complete your end of the bargain."

"Have no fear on that account." Meredith smiled. "I look forward to meeting the young man. What was his name? Christopher? After an initial introduction, I'll let you know if I'll be able to assist you in this matter." She took another sip of her tea, letting Whitby know by her manner that he was dismissed. She'd long ago learned if one acted like royalty, one was likely to be treated as such.

"Good. Very well then, madame. I will arrange a meeting. Where would you like it to take place, a dinner party, a ball, or something more intimate? I must say, it's rather difficult to get the boy to commit to any social event."

"Invite me to a light tea on Friday." She imagined her target would be more relaxed in his natural environment, and she could better assess his personality, his interests and his strengths and weaknesses.

Whitby rose and bowed. "Thank you. I may, of course, count on your discretion should you choose not to...exchange favors?"

The countess laughed lightly. "Certainly. How would I profit from letting it be known you asked me to make a man of your son?"

"Yes, well..." He cleared his throat. "Good day, madame. I shall tell my wife to send an invitation for Friday."

As she watched him walk from the room, she wondered how he would explain to his wife the sudden need for them to befriend the infamous Comtesse de Chevalier. Only her connection to nobility allowed her entrée into society despite the rumors of her scandalous, outrageous behavior.

Most of the stories weren't rumors; the bacchanalian parties at her country estate, the affairs with gentlemen and occasionally women, the encounters with whomever caught her fancy, from a head of state to a common laborer. The countess was egalitarian in her sexual proclivities. She indulged in far more decadence than prudish society even imagined. Charming and seducing a bookish man was not going to be a problem. By the time she finished with Christopher, he would be a work of art. Any woman lucky enough to land him would never know that she had the la Comtesse de Chevalier to thank for her pleasure.

Chapter Two

"How in the world could it possibly matter if I'm present for tea with this Countess whoever?" *And since when does Father take an interest in whether I come or go?* Chris drew a deep breath, unable to fill his lungs properly in the over-heated, stifling den. He'd never been comfortable in this dark-paneled room and empathized deeply with the stuffed elk head on the wall, killed and mounted for a gentleman's sporting décor. Father hadn't even shot the elk, but bought the head at an estate sale.

"Will you, for once, do what I request? For that matter, this isn't a request, but a command. You *will* come to tea and make your mother happy!" Father's voice rose on the last words.

There was something odd about the situation, but Chris couldn't imagine what was going through his father's mind. "I've already made plans. There's a lecture at the Botanical Gardens on the *Ayapana triplinervis*. Professor Einrich Lufkin is presenting samples from his recent South American expedition."

"You can go to your flower exhibit another time. Today I insist you attend tea with our honored guest."

"This is a once in a lifetime opportunity. I won't miss it." Chris usually avoided arguments by simply staying out of his father's way and following his own desires, but today the man was making it impossible to avoid confrontation.

"What time? When is this ridiculous professor speaking?"

"At six o'clock."

"Tea is at four. You should be able to attend your lecture afterward."

Chris couldn't argue with that logic, and was beginning to be almost curious about why his father was so insistent on his meeting this countess.

"Very well. I shall stay for tea."

Thus it was that a couple of hours later he found himself in a high, starched collar and throat-choking cravat, wearing a coat that was far too warm for such a fine afternoon. He'd escaped the house to spend time in his garden before he was called on to make polite conversation with a stranger over tea. If the countess was such an illustrious guest, shouldn't his mother be fluttering in nervous anticipation instead of wearing a sour face? The invitation appeared to be a grudging one on her part, which made no sense given that his mother usually enjoyed entertaining. But then his parents' motivations were often a mystery to him.

Plants were much easier to relate to than people, who talked and talked but said nothing of any value. He bent to examine the Thornescroft hybrid he'd so carefully cultivated all season long. The first rose would soon open and he eagerly anticipated the event, doing everything in his power to keep the aphids and beetles at bay lest they devour the leaves and chew holes in the blossom.

He touched the bud with his fingertip. The soft pink petals were pressed tightly closed and waiting to unfurl. Nature was endlessly fascinating in its complexity and infinite beauty.

"Christopher." His father's voice broke into his reverie. "Our guest has arrived. Please welcome Madame la Comtesse de Chevalier."

Chris straightened and squinted against the blinding light, trying to focus on the features of the woman standing on the steps above the garden path. How very odd that Father should escort her to the garden. Mother's friends always remained inside, out of the hot sun, and visiting ladies usually merited little attention from his father.

Recalling his manners, Chris strode forward and held out his hand. "How do you do, Madame la Comtesse." He was pleased he'd remembered to use her title as was appropriate. Since he generally shunned the social whirl, it was easy to forget such protocol.

"Pleased to meet you, Mr. Whitby." Her cool hand slid into his and he noticed it was ungloved, most unusual for a lady. The smooth skin sent a pleasant tingling charge into his palm. He'd moved so the sun wasn't blinding him and now could see her face, which caused him to pause with her hand still clutched in his.

Her eyes were the color of the sky on a cloudy day and fringed in deep black lashes that reminded him of the thick petals of some exotic flower. That image was enhanced by the scent of her spicy, foreign perfume, which wafted around him and made him think of India, a place he'd never been but would like to visit. Her shiny black hair, piled in elaborate loops and curls, also conjured fantasies of distant lands. She might have been a Maharani in a sari rather than the English widow of a French count repatriated to her native land.

Her royal blue dress seemed too rich and vibrant for an afternoon tea. It was the color of a rare orchid he'd once seen and nothing like the insipid pastels that women usually wore in the daytime. Chris didn't know much about fashion, but guessed this was more the hue of an evening dress. Her lack of convention, paired with a certain pride of bearing, informed him that Madame de Chevalier was what society termed "eccentric". For that, he liked her already.

She smiled, her rose petal lips parting to reveal even, white teeth. Her cool gray eyes sparkled with merriment, and he liked her even more.

"You're a botanist, Mr. Whitby? I'd love to take a stroll through your garden, if I may."

Really? Her proposal surprised him. None of his mother's other friends had ever expressed an interest in the garden.

"Certainly." He remembered to offer his arm as she lifted her skirt in one hand and walked down the two shallow steps leading to the garden.

Lord Whitby cleared his throat. "I've a few matters to attend to so I'll leave you to your walk." He disappeared back into the house and Chris was left to entertain the countess.

Although her hand rested lightly on his arm, he could feel the weight of it even through his jacket. Curious, how it was so warm and made his pulse beat faster. The sun seemed hotter than ever and sweat prickled on his neck beneath his collar. Oh, how he longed to tear off the offensive cravat and breathe freely.

"These roses are lovely. What variety are they?" she asked, releasing his arm and stooping to touch a pink bud.

"Thornescroft. It's a cultivated hybrid." He went on to explain how roses were bred, but stopped after several minutes lest he bore her.

The countess straightened from examining the rose and glanced at him. "Go on. I never realized the time and effort that went into creating different varieties. It's fascinating."

Chris detected no sarcasm in her tone so he continued to explain about grafting processes as they strolled along the row of bushes. He concluded his explanation, and then added, "Roses are interesting, but they're not my passion."

"What is?" She stopped walking and turned to him. With her erect carriage and high-piled hair she'd seemed quite tall and imposing when standing on the step above him. But as she looked up into his eyes from only a foot away, he realized she was petite and her bone structure very delicate. A rush of heat swept through him and he damned the sun for being so hot.

For a moment he couldn't speak. He'd forgotten what he was saying and had to search for the thread of his thought. Flowers. Plants. Passion. Ah, yes. "I would give anything to travel to China and see *Incarvillea mairei* or *Ferula olivacia* first hand. Artists' renderings aren't like viewing the plants in their natural habitat. How I should love to stand on a mountain slope and see *Gentiana* spread in a blue carpet across the hillside." He smiled, almost smelling the clear mountain air and seeing the breathtaking vista.

"Why can't you go?" Her voice was soft.

He knew it was inappropriate to discuss his finances, but her sympathetic eyes encouraged him to tell the truth. "Unfortunately, I lack the necessary funds. My bequest from my grandfather coupled with my allowance is enough for me to continue my studies, but hardly to travel at great length. I intend to take a position at Cambridge in the Natural Science department and hopefully I can get a grant to pursue my research abroad. My father doesn't know this yet."

"I should think he would be proud to have a professor in the family."

Chris smiled. "Not unless the professor was also a sportsman or a great cricket player. I'm afraid I don't fit my father's ideal of what a man should be." The words spilled from his lips. He didn't know why he was sharing all this with a complete stranger, but the woman's eyes continued to draw him out and pull him in. A man could get lost in such mysterious, misty gray eyes.

He shrugged and looked away to break the spell. "At any rate, those are my plans. And this"—he indicated the profusion of plants and shrubs surrounding them—"is my town garden. I prefer to spend more time at our country estate where I have a large greenhouse and nearly an acre of gardens to supervise, but I must reside near the university for now."

Chris continued walking the pathway with the countess beside him.

"Speaking of country estates," she said. "I have a conservatory of my own that has been sorely neglected. I've considered hiring someone to put it in order, but haven't gotten around to it." She rested a hand on his forearm, stopping him. "Do you think you could possibly find the time to spend a few weeks at my home? I would love professional advice on the best plants to cultivate and perhaps a design for the space."

"I..." He hardly knew how to answer. It was an unusual request, but he was his own man now, with his degree completed and his future plans not yet implemented. He had time at his disposal. "I suppose I could visit for a while. I should enjoy helping you create a working greenhouse."

She smiled and clapped her hands together. "Marvelous! I'm sure together we can entice some life out of the barren soil. It shall be an experiment neither of us will ever forget."

Chris frowned, feeling her words held some hidden meaning, but he supposed he simply wasn't used to the way women expressed themselves. He was around them so seldom. "Yes. It should be lovely," he replied.

The countess hooked her hand over his arm, sending another warm tingle through him as he escorted her into the house for tea.

ဆ

The lecture on South American plants was long and full of even longer Latin words. Meredith suppressed a yawn as the lecturer droned on. The colorful illustrations his assistant placed on the tripod broke the monotony a little, but she found herself trying to count how many of them were still to be displayed. If each picture prompted a five minute explanation, then it looked like there may be as many as forty-five minutes left in this lecture. If there was some kind of concluding speech, they could easily be here another hour.

She glanced at her companion, Christopher Whitby, and smiled at the avid expression on his face, his gleaming blue eyes and slightly parted lips. He was as entranced with the lecture as she was bored. While he had shown her his garden and talked about the plants, she'd found his enthusiasm about his chosen field of study endearing. His informal air and self-effacing presence was charming, and his features were handsome in an understated way.

His hair was tousled, but not in the styled manner that society rakes arranged their curls. Christopher's was naturally messy. Sandy brown locks fell over his forehead, and she longed to ruffle her hand through his hair. A sweet ache and a hot flash of lust swelled simultaneously in her breast.

The man appeared more boyish than his years, but in the hard planes of his face and the set of his jaw, Meredith detected the strong-willed man he had the capability of being. In the few hours since she'd met him, Christopher's eyes had often appeared unfocused and dreamy as if he were somewhere other than sitting at a tea table engaged in stilted conversation. Yet when he'd talked directly to her in the garden, he'd been engaged and focused. Power and energy flowed from his piercing eyes and vibrated from his body. She had no doubt this passion channeled into lovemaking would be formidable.

It had been easy to engineer an invitation to accompany him to the presentation at the Royal Botanical Gardens and, honestly, she was quite intrigued by the prospect. She'd envisioned walking in the fragrant, tropical warmth of exotic climates protected by the glass bubble. She hadn't counted on the lecture being so very long and dull. But, she'd already decided to take on Lord Whitby's proposition, and the first step to gaining her new lover was to show an interest in what fascinated him.

Meredith didn't generally believe in operating on

pretense. She'd given that up after her husband's death, when his money had freed her from society's constraints and she'd finally begun living life by her own rules. She no longer had to feign interest in every little thing a man said or did. That wasn't necessary in order to gain what she wanted from them. But she did try to at least understand the passions that made them tick, whether they were hunting, gaming, business, politics or books. She'd learned a little about all things considered masculine and could readily converse on any subject of interest to her paramours.

"Have you heard enough?" A low whisper and faint brush of warm breath against her cheek roused Meredith from her reverie.

She glanced at her escort. He leaned toward her, his face mere inches away, brow furrowed and blue eyes peering into hers. She had a sudden impulse to lean in and kiss him, to replace his look of anxious concern with one of shock and desire.

"I wouldn't mind a stroll," she murmured.

Christopher rose from his seat, took her hand and helped her to her feet. Together they made their way down the nearly empty row of seats to the door of the lecture hall.

The conservatories were nearly empty so late in the evening and lit by flickering gaslights casting strange, leaf-shaped shadows that eerily shifted and moved. As they passed from the arid climate of the desert room to the damp humidity of the tropical garden, it was like entering an alien, green world from which a jungle beast might suddenly leap. The humid air was dense and redolent of earth and growing things.

Meredith's kid shoes crunched on the white gravel path and her dress clung to her perspiring skin. She would've liked to strip it off and wander through the palm fronds and ferns in a diaphanous gauze gown like some preternatural dryad.

"I can see why you love them," she said to Christopher, who strode silently by her side. "The plants, I mean. It's so peaceful here." She spoke in a reverent hush as though in a church.

"Nature truly gives one a glimpse into the mystery of the universe. To the untrained eye, plants might appear to be just a lot of green leaves and pretty flowers, but the structure of each is unique. Each has adapted in miraculous ways to survive in its environment." He stopped and rested a hand on the bark of a towering tree, the canopy of which brushed the fogged glass high overhead.

"They're like people in that regard," Meredith said, moving in close beside him. "Each of us has to adapt to our world in various ways, don't we?"

When he turned to look at her, she was right there. She tilted her head back and offered him an invitation with her eyes, curious as to whether he would accept it. His tongue swept over his lips, but he remained poised, inches away, with his gaze trained on her mouth.

This was early in the game to make a bold move. She

didn't want to frighten her quarry away, but that ripe lower lip was too inviting to ignore. She raised her hand and cupped the side of his face, tracing her thumb over his mouth. "Shall we take a small detour from the path?"

His eyes were wide and shining, his breathing uneven and shallow. Silently, he nodded.

The countess took her hand from his face and grasped his warm palm in hers. "Come, then." They walked from the main path toward a bench secluded in a grove of trees and screened by some kind of flowering vine.

He gripped her hand and followed her like an obedient child. But he wasn't a child, and his first lesson in becoming a man would begin this evening.

80

The onslaught of sensations, the racing pulse, ragged breathing, prickling skin, heightened senses and burgeoning heat in his cock took Chris completely by surprise. It wasn't as though he'd never felt any of these things. He was an adult male with a man's lust and yearning when he caught sight of a pretty face, deep cleavage or a flash of ankle, but he'd never felt such a tumult of emotion all at once. All because Madame de Chevalier had touched his lips and peered into his very thoughts with her wise gray eyes.

He couldn't be imagining this, could he? Perhaps he'd

fallen asleep during the professor's lecture and was dreaming this erotic encounter. But the solidity of the cool stone bench beneath his trousers and the warmth of the lady's hand in his assured him the moment was very real.

Once seated on the bench, she turned her body toward his and again reached to stroke the side of his face. Her fingers were cool and soft as silk, and his eyes closed part way in response to her touch. She slid her hand around the back of his neck and encouraged him to lean toward her. It was actually happening—a kiss, something he'd fantasized but had pushed to the back of his mind because it didn't fit into his plans for a life devoted to academic study.

Tilting his head slightly, he closed his eyes completely as her face loomed closer. Sightless, his mouth found and covered hers. Their lips pressed together and he couldn't suppress the quiet moan that rose in his throat. Her lips were soft and yielding. He pressed hard against them. A kiss. His first kiss—embarrassing to admit at age twenty-five, but there'd been no opportunity before now. He wouldn't steal favors from a housemaid as some men did, and young ladies didn't bestow kisses until an engagement ring was offered. The one chance he'd had to experience mindless pleasure was with a prostitute, a gift from his father that Chris simply couldn't accept.

Ah, but he would indulge now with a woman he barely knew. A friend of his mother's no less. What kind of woman was the countess that she kissed strange men on a whim? Christopher stopped thinking and focused on the moment, the feel of her waist beneath his hand as he slipped it around her, the yielding softness of her mouth beneath his and the mounting pressure in his cock as it strained against his breeches.

The countess pressed a hand against his chest and pulled away. Chris wanted to reach for her blindly and pull her back again. He nearly whined at the interruption, but instead opened his eyes to look into her face. "I-I'm sorry. I was wrong to…"

"No. Sh." She covered his lips with her finger, then stroked them with her fingertip. "Not that. I want to show you a little something about kissing.

"Oh." He resisted the impulse to suck her finger right into his mouth and waited while she slid the tip back and forth across his lips until they tingled.

"When you kiss a woman, you must think of her lips as a flower, a bud which you're seducing into opening for you. Light, delicate strokes of the tongue, soft pressure of the lips are the keys to making that flower bloom. Understand?"

Her analogy was wrong. There was nothing a person could do to make a flower open. It happened when it was time. But he understood her meaning and blushed, realizing his technique had been off. Mashing his mouth hard against hers clearly hadn't been satisfying for her. He nodded.

Her shining eyes continued to gaze into his and her hypnotic finger to stroke his parted lips and dip just barely between them. He dared to touch it with the tip of his tongue and a ripple of something passed over the countess's eyes. She made a small sound.

"Yes. Keep your lips relaxed, moist but not wet, and tease mine into opening for you. Then we shall see what will follow." Her thick, dark lashes swept her cheeks in lush fans as her eyes closed and her face lifted toward his.

Chris took his time. He touched her face as she had his, stroking her soft cheek and jaw, caressing her mouth until her pink lips parted. Then he rested his hand on her throat and felt the pulse beating in it like butterfly wings. He slid his hand around her neck and let it rest under the base of her skull, supporting her. The hairs at her nape tickled the back of his hand. He inclined his head and kissed her again.

This time he followed her instruction, feeding at her lips as a hummingbird sips nectar. Closing his mouth over her pouting lower lip, he pulled on it lightly. He pressed little nibbling kisses to the corners of her mouth and then slipped his tongue over the seam of her lips. They opened as she gave a small gasp of pleasure. His tongue slipped inside the heat and moisture of her mouth and encountered her tongue, slippery and sinuous. The percolating heat in his belly flared to an inferno from this simple touch. A raging beast was awakened, which Chris recognized as the primitive animal inside every man. He ached to devour her, to kiss her until she couldn't breathe, to throw her down on the ground and ravish her.

His soft, exploratory kiss grew harder and more demanding. His tongue swept inside her mouth, tasting her and filling her just as his cock ached to fill her body.

29

The powerful intensity of animal emotion was overwhelming. His penis throbbed with each beat of his heart and he was afraid it would explode into his drawers. With a low groan, he released her waist and the back of her neck, gripped her shoulders and pushed her away.

Gasping, he gazed into her suddenly wide-open eyes. "We must stop now." He rose abruptly from the bench, stumbling backward and treading on a sample of *Floribunda segunda* before quickly stepping away from it.

"This is too..." He trailed off, not knowing how to express his thoughts. *Too powerful. Too intense and real. Too dangerous.*

She smiled up at him. "Christopher, don't be alarmed. I'm a widow. In our society, widows may take their pleasure where they wish, as long as they're discreet."

He waved a hand at the bower of trees and flowers around them. "This is hardly discreet. We're in the Royal Botanical Gardens."

The countess stood, and he took another step back. "Would you feel more comfortable elsewhere?" she asked. "We could go to my house."

"I..." Good Christ! The woman was stunning, regal, elegant, beautiful, and asking him to come to her home. Her invitation left little to the imagination. What could possibly hold him back? Any man would jump at the chance to share la Comtesse de Chevalier's bed. "I must go now." His voice was a hoarse mutter.

Without another word, he turned and walked away, buttoning his jacket over the bulge in his breeches. A torrent of emotions, which he tried to tame into submission, raged through him. Science and reason had always been the guiding forces of his life. Animal impulses were for uneducated, unthinking louts. There must be more to life than satisfying base lust with bestial coupling; otherwise the whole of society might as well run about in animal skins cooking shanks of meat over open fires.

Besides, if he once gave into passion, Chris didn't know if he'd ever be able to return to the person he'd been before. And if he wasn't that man, the quiet, reserved man who studied and raised plants, then who was he?

Chapter Three

Meredith lounged in her peignoir in the salon of her country home, reading a racing form, a black cheroot clamped between her teeth. Wisps of smoke wafted from the thin cigar to wreathe her head. She didn't really care much for smoking, but the cigar was a ritual for her, a device she used to recall her dead husband, le Comte de Chevalier. Like the carved tusk on her mantle, it was her touchstone, something to remind her of the man who'd shaped her life and ultimately given her freedom. It was also a tribute to the girl she'd been and a statement about the weakness and vulnerability she'd left behind.

As a young bride of seventeen, she'd wed the count and left her parents' home to move to France. It was an advantageous marriage for her family, since her father had inherited a title, an estate and little else. Stephan had spied young Meredith at the first ball of the Season and claimed her within the week. Swept off her feet by the charming, attractive older man, Meredith had readily agreed to his proposal. Her mother was overjoyed and immediately began trumpeting to anyone who would listen about the marvelous match her daughter had made.

Meredith remembered how nervous yet exhilarated she'd been at the prospect of marriage. She'd only just left the tutelage of her governess. Barely launched into society, she was already chosen. Romantic fancies of what married life would be like spun out in her mind, fueled by novels she kept hidden in her room.

The reality of the marriage bed had been a harsh awakening.

The count had bedded her roughly the first time, nearly tearing her clothes off in his haste to see her naked, then plunging into her fast and hard. She was dry, not at all prepared for his entry, and it hurt. He grunted and thrust like an animal. When his lust was sated, he rolled off of her, put on a dressing gown and paused in the doorway to look back at her, curled into a ball on the rumpled covers.

"You shall get used to it, *ma petite*. It only hurts the first time."

He was wrong. The count never waited for her to become slick with anticipation, and always used her hard and rough as if she were a whore instead of a wife. He seemed to get great satisfaction from her pain and often grasped her hair and twisted it while he pumped into her. He murmured French phrases she'd never learned from her governess, which she imagined were obscenities, and pinched, squeezed and slapped her at random.

Over the course of a few days, he fucked her a dozen times, then announced he was leaving for a hunting expedition in Africa. He left her behind in his vast chateau under the watchful eye of Madame Baillon, who he told her would see to all her needs. The woman was a guardian to make sure she didn't try to go home to her parents or entertain male visitors while the count was abroad. There was no wedding tour as promised, just a young girl abandoned in a vast, echoing house with servants who clearly resented her English ways and made her feel powerless and young.

Meredith spent days crying and barely leaving her room, before she shook off her bitterness and despair and decided to make the best of the situation. She walked the gardens and grounds with Baillon always just behind her. She attempted to meet ladies from the neighboring homes. They were barely polite. The French hatred for all things British kept her always an outsider in their society.

When the count returned home after several months, he brought her the carved tusk, and a renewed onslaught of sexual abuse and mounting degradation. At least, when he was home, they were invited to social events so there was something to fill the long, empty days. But she was very grateful after a few months, when her husband announced he was leaving again, this time on a trip to South America.

That had been the sum of her marriage, a series of long, lonely stretches of time followed by assault and mounting violence from the stranger she'd chosen to marry. He grew increasingly angry when she didn't conceive, and his temper exploded through his fists and cock. He began to use her even harder and to experiment with perverse tortures and bondage, all the while heaping verbal abuse upon her.

Several years into the marriage, Meredith began to consider whether dying might not be preferable to her miserable life. But instead, she fired Madame Baillon while the count was away on one of his expeditions and dared to take her life into her own hands, sailing to England and leasing a house in London. Perhaps Stephan would come after her and drag her home. Perhaps there would be repercussions for her escape, but at least she was trying to make a change.

Meredith never found out how her husband would have reacted. She received news that he'd died of malaria. Since he'd left no heir to inherit the estate, a distant cousin took possession of it, but Meredith was left with a considerable income and her freedom.

Over the next few years she concentrated on translating the bequeathed money into a small fortune, ensuring she'd never again be dependent on any man. Business became her passion. She loved to watch her investments and holdings grow.

Only in the past five years had she finally come to an appreciation of other passions. At age thirty-one she'd met a man who showed her lovemaking could be pleasurable and fulfilling. A series of sexual adventures and experiments followed, and the countess gained a notorious reputation. She was someone a respectable woman would prefer not to invite to tea, but her title gained her admittance into society. Meredith lived in a strange limbo, as she had all her life, with no real friends or confidantes, merely an endless succession of lovers and social events to attend. In many ways, she was as lonely as she had been when floating around the count's chateau all those years ago.

With an irritated sigh at her melancholy, she leaned forward to crush out the barely smoked cheroot and close the racing form. She rang a bell, summoning Hawkins, her butler, and told him on which horse to place her bet. This was one of her little vices, a weekly gamble. She would never endanger her fortune by playing with a serious amount, but enjoyed the excitement and possibility of a small bet.

Of course, there was nothing more invigorating than gambling on a human being. When she'd promised Lord Whitby she would take on the case of his son, she was fairly certain she'd already won Christopher over. He might take a little persuasion, but would eventually succumb to her. It was the process of seducing him that was thrilling.

The kisses in the Botanical Gardens had been an exceedingly pleasant diversion. Feeling the change in him from awkward boy to aggressive man, from inexperienced, closed-mouthed presses of his lips to the hot, thrusting of his tongue... A shiver ran through her at the memory. She was entranced by the idea of taking his virginity, of teaching him about passion and revealing to him the side of himself he'd denied for far too long. As a matter of fact, she couldn't wait to begin.

After Christopher had left her that night in the Gardens, she'd sent a note asking him to consider her request to visit her country estate. A day of silence had followed before he'd replied. "I accept your kind invitation and would enjoy examining your plants. C. Whitby."

She had smiled on reading the somehow suggestive words, certain that he'd been completely innocent of any extra meaning when composing them. Or maybe he was aware of exactly what her invitation meant and unconsciously answered with words that expressed his true feelings. He'd like very much to examine her plants.

Now, as she awaited Chris Whitby's arrival at her country home, she smiled again, eager for the fun to start. If a mere kiss or two had stirred her, imagine the fireworks in store when passion was really ignited. This young man was exactly what she needed to bring some zest to her jaded palate. Experiencing sex with a virgin would make it new for her as well. And she'd ensure his experience was far more pleasant than her first time had been—memorable in a good way.

Meredith summoned her maid to help her dress for the day in a buttercup morning gown that made a sunny contrast to her black hair and peach skin. Cecile brushed her hair, while Meredith sat plotting her seduction. She'd chosen the yellow because it was a sweet, youthful color. Today she wanted to present the picture of an innocent country maiden. She eschewed wearing any of her jewelry and had Cecile keep her hair down, twisting only a small knot at the back of her head. Tumbling ringlets added to the fresh-faced appeal she was promoting.

She'd rushed Christopher too quickly last time, counting on nature to take its course and not taking into account whatever demons held him back from acknowledging his sexuality. This time she'd use her wiles, find out what kept him from fulfilling his natural inclinations and loosen the knots that bound him.

A light spray of floral perfume completed her toilette and then, before she had time to begin fretting or fidgeting, she heard the sound of a carriage rolling to a halt on the drive in front of the house. She stood behind the curtain in the window of her salon and watched Whitby step down from the carriage and gaze up at the house. She felt she could see the intense blue of his eyes even from this distance.

Servants carried his bags indoors and Christopher followed, squaring his shoulders as if he were going to meet the guillotine instead of a beautiful woman.

Meredith turned from the window, checked her face once more in the looking glass, then walked down the hallway. She descended the main staircase slowly and regally. The moment she saw Christopher standing in the foyer, she fixed her gaze on his, holding him with her eyes as surely as if she embraced him in her arms.

After a quick scan of her body, his bright eyes focused on hers. His posture was erect, back stiff, hands at his sides with the fingers lightly clenched.

She appreciated the classic style and somber brown of his coat and tan breeches. Too many men were peacocks in garish, contrasting colors these days with cravats that held their chins so high they looked like show ponies. Whitby's restrained style was much more attractive. The simple cut of his clothes accentuated the long lines of his body. She imagined what he looked like naked—not incredibly muscular since he didn't, according to his father, pursue any sport, but probably lean and taut nonetheless. With any luck, she would know the answer in a day or two. From the way he was devouring her with his eyes, maybe sooner.

"Good afternoon, Mr. Whitby. I trust your journey was uneventful." She extended her hand as she approached him.

He bowed, took her hand and pressed his lips quickly to the back of it. "Very."

"Are you hungry? I've arranged for a light luncheon. It will be served on the veranda. If you'd like to refresh yourself first, Hawkins will show you to your room."

Half an hour later, he joined her at the table under the shade of the awning that protected them from the glorious sunshine. An assortment of fresh fruit and canapés were arrayed on silver trays. "Would you like something a little more filling?" she asked as he took his seat. "My cook can make you a full meal."

"No. This is sufficient. I don't often eat at midday." Christopher sat stiffly with his hands in his lap. His eyes scanned the gardens beyond the veranda, then came back to rest on her face. "Very beautiful," he offered, and for a moment, she wasn't sure if he meant the gardens or her.

"Yes. I'm embarrassed to say that, unlike you, I have nothing to do with my gardens. Not even the choice of plants, I'm afraid. I've left it all to my gardener. You'll have to tell me if he's done well. They look all right to me, but I'm no expert." As she spoke, she prepared a plate and placed it in front of him, then poured tea for them both. "You must tell me what prompted your interest in plants."

A quick smile like summer lightning flashed across his mouth, then disappeared. "I suppose I've always liked plants because they're so...restful. There's nothing like a walk in nature to soothe one's soul and put the manmade world into perspective. There's an order and simplicity in nature that mankind has lost sight of." He lifted his teacup and sipped.

Meredith was surprised at his candor and the depth of his answer. She'd often taken long walks to put her life into perspective. Of course, she'd usually been working through problems in her head rather than taking in the beauty of the landscape, but his point was well made. "You find humans full of artifice?"

"Not in primitive native tribes, but in European society, most definitely. Our society is based on acquisitiveness and the presumption that advancing financially or socially is the purpose of existence. People have deceived themselves about their true nature."

"Which is...?" She was intrigued to know what he would say. For a man who believed in the natural order of things, he certainly seemed out of touch with his own primal nature and the passions and lusts that drove the human animal.

He dipped his head, gazing at a strawberry on his plate. "I've spoken too much. I'm afraid I don't often get a chance to share my thoughts, and it has made me speak inappropriately."

"On the contrary, Mr. Whitby, I'm fascinated by your views, and there's nothing you can say that will cause me shock or disapproval. I agree that our society is based on deception and hypocrisy. I would have you always speak plainly to me, for I am as open to new ideas as I imagine you are."

Christopher paused with the strawberry lifted halfway to his mouth and stared at her. "I've never heard a woman speak so honestly."

"Trust me, *monsieur*, I am not most women. I'm considered more than a little eccentric."

"Then how in the world did my mother come to invite you to tea?" His cheeks flushed and he set the berry down. "Pardon me for such a rude question, but my mother is most conservative. I don't quite understand how she befriended you."

Meredith considered her answer. Clearly the arrangement with his father couldn't be mentioned, but remaining close to the truth would be best. "In all honesty, I am not a particular friend of your mother's. Your father bade her invite me so I might meet you."

"Father? Why in the world would he do that, and why in the world would you come?"

Here's where her explanation got complicated and required an actual lie or at least a warped version of the truth. "I'd seen you before—at the ball given last month by Lord and Lady Atwater. Do you recall?"

"I recall being coerced into attending by my mother, but I don't remember seeing you there, and I believe I would. You make rather an impression."

"It was a well-attended event. I wouldn't expect you to have noticed me in the throng, but I noticed you."

His eyebrows shot up in disbelief. "I can't imagine why."

"Because you were so still and quiet, a great contrast to the blustering, loud gentlemen trying to gain my attention. I thought you were a person to whom it would be interesting to speak. Before I could go over and do so, you left. I approached your father, whom I knew through a mutual acquaintance, and asked for an introduction that I might come to know you better."

Bits of the truth were in there. She actually did remember someone mentioning the Whitbys' hopelessly socially inept son that evening at the ball as they pointed out Christopher skulking near a potted plant, but that was all the impression he'd made on her at that time.

"Pardon me for saying that sounds rather preposterous." The lightning smile came and went again. "I know I'm not that memorable of a person."

"Nevertheless, you made an impression on me." She reached across the table, took the strawberry from his plate and lifted it to his mouth, both her hand and her eyes offering something.

Christopher licked his lips as he regarded the berry. He slowly opened his mouth and Meredith just as slowly placed it inside, making sure her fingers brushed his tongue and touched his lips as she did so. She smiled. "You must think I'm a most forward and provocative woman, but when I find something I want, I reach for it."

His mouth closed and his jaw worked as he chewed the berry, then swallowed it. "I can well believe that." His voice was hoarse when he spoke. "But I simply don't understand how you could possibly be interested in me."

"Mm." She smiled and sat back in her chair, lifting her own cup of tea and sipping it as she searched for an answer. She was happy to be able to speak the truth.

"It has to do with what you said about humans having lost touch with their natural side. Mankind's true nature is quite bestial underneath all the trappings of a civilized society." She pressed her hand to her breast. "In here we have strong passions and desires that can't be denied, only controlled to a degree. Who knows what stirs them and why? I saw you and wanted you. It's that simple."

He stared at her, frowning.

Meredith released him from her gaze and returned the conversation to more mundane channels, giving him time to digest her words. "Enough talking for now. You must try my cook Genevieve's marvelous canapés and biscuits or her feelings will be hurt and then God knows what she shall serve us for dinner."

Christopher seemed relieved to turn his attention to his plate. He must have been quite hungry from the journey because he emptied it while she talked about how she'd come to purchase her house.

"After my husband died and I moved back to England,

I was happy to live in London for a while, but one beautiful afternoon I decided I'd had enough of coal smoke shrouding the air and filling my lungs. This estate was for sale, the last remaining Barrington having died childless, and I was able to purchase it. When we're finished eating I shall show you around both inside and out. I'm very proud of all the improvements I've made."

"How long were you married, if I may ask? You seem so young to be a widow."

"Three years, which was quite sufficient given my husband's disposition, and I'm not as young as you might think."

"How... Forgive me." He blushed, revealing he'd been about to ask her age.

"Older than you." She smiled, enjoying giving him a little mystery to puzzle over. "And wiser I shouldn't wonder. Perhaps I can teach you a few things after you teach me how to care for my plants." She gave a suggestive pause, then added as a joke. "For instance, I could teach you to play whist unless you already know how."

He didn't respond, clearly uncertain how to tease and flirt. Well, she would teach him to do that, too, before she was through with him.

"Come now." She rose to her feet, returning to the pretense that he was here merely to help her with her gardening problem. "Why don't I show you my conservatory and you can tell me how to bring it back to life?" Lifting her skirts, she led the way from the veranda around the side of the house to the large glass enclosure she'd ignored since occupying the house.

She unlatched and opened the door. Heat flowed from the unventilated room in a choking cloud. Walking into it was like entering a dry desert. "Oh, my. I should have had Klaus open it up to air out. It's stifling."

Christopher followed her inside. She turned to him and saw beads of perspiration already shining on his forehead. Sweat prickled on her face, too, and she fanned it. "I told you the room had been neglected."

Together they surveyed the nearly empty building. A few dead potted trees huddled in one corner. Shelves intended for seedlings held only empty flats with powdery dirt in them. A dry fountain was the centerpiece of a slate path. Shreds of paint clung to a wooden bench, which sat just off the path. Once it may have been sheltered in a bower of green leaves, but now it squatted on bare earth.

Meredith held up her hands, indicating the parched ground, devoid of life. "You see? I wouldn't know where to begin."

Christopher nodded as he took off his jacket, loosened his plain cravat and rolled up his sleeves. He didn't seem to notice her any longer as he took stock of the building, walking up and down its length and opening windows and the overhead vents. He lifted a handful of soil and examined it closely before letting it sift through his fingers. Meredith was fascinated by the way the muscles moved in his forearms. They looked good with the sleeves rolled up, tanned and with a fine down of hair.

He strode past her to stand before the shelving, testing the strength of the boards to see if any had rotted. Meredith might as well have been invisible for all the notice he took of her now that he was focused on the project. Her yellow dress, so crisp and fresh that morning, clung to her damp body now, as did the layers of undergarments she longed to shed. What would he do if she did just that—stripped one layer after another?

She smiled at the notion. He would probably ignore her nudity and keep right on assessing the merits of climbing vines versus cacti. Standing quietly aside, she watched him work.

Finally Christopher acknowledged her. "Do you have anything to write with? I'd like to make a list, and then I can draw up a plan to show you what I have in mind."

"No. I'm afraid I didn't come prepared." She brushed back damp tendrils of hair that clung to her forehead. "But perhaps we should go in the house now. I can provide you with what you need and, more importantly, we can cool down."

"It is a trifle warm."

"Just a trifle." *Too hot for a seduction.*

She opened the door and led the way into the relative coolness of the late-summer day. The breeze carried the scent of honeysuckle from the trellised vines near the greenhouse. The sweet aroma was a contrast to the dry, dusty smell inside the glass enclosure. Meredith imagined what it would be like when green life once more filled the conservatory, when she could sit by the fountain in the dead of winter and read a book. Although the renovation had begun as a ruse to get Christopher to her house, she began to be excited by the prospect.

Walking swiftly to keep up with his long strides, she glanced at the young man beside her. What an unusual person he was, a potent mixture of keen intelligence and shy self-effacement mingled with an earthy sensuality that lurked beneath the surface. Meredith had no doubt his primal side could curl a woman's toes once she'd tapped it. She'd felt the hunger when he kissed her the other night and it should be easy to rouse it again. A frisson of excitement tickled her insides at the prospect.

They entered the house by the kitchen door and paused to clean up at the sink. Meredith washed her hands and face and smoothed back her hair, then dried herself on a towel as she watched Christopher do the same. It was completely improper to make ablutions in front of one another as though they were common laborers. The very informality was erotic. Water dripped from his forearms and elbows, wetting his rolled up sleeves as he splashed water on his face. His sandy hair darkened where it was damp.

After he'd straightened from the sink and dried his face, Meredith stepped close and combed her fingers through the wet-spiked tendrils. "Blind ninnies," she murmured, gazing up into his eyes a foot above hers.

"Pardon?" The word was choked and he swallowed hard as though his throat was too dry for speaking.

"Society chits. How many chances have those young

ladies had at balls and parties to try to snag you? But they didn't see what was in front of them."

A little smile tilted the corners of his mouth. "Actually, I've had my share of interest. I'm the sole heir of my father's fortune and our name is respected."

"Hm. Those women saw a title only. They didn't see you." Without planning to, she rose up on her toes and kissed him. He gave a slight gasp as her mouth covered his. She pressed against his overheated body, and his hands automatically went to her waist, steadying her. Meredith's hands slid around his hot neck and pulled his head down that she might kiss him even more deeply. All her intentions to entice him to her bed by slow measures were gone. A flash of hot lust burst through her, and she wanted to take him right there in the kitchen amidst Genevieve's pots and pans.

She forgot her own kissing lessons and attacked his mouth rather than teasing it to response. Christopher didn't seem to have a problem with that. His hands roamed up and down her back, trying to touch her everywhere at once, although they stopped short of crossing her waistline to cup her bottom. His tongue tangled with hers and explored her mouth. Their teeth clicked together with the force of their kiss, and when Meredith finally pulled away to suck in a breath of air, she was lightheaded.

Christopher was panting, too. His chest rose and fell. His lips were parted and damp. His wide eyes were dilated so dark they appeared navy instead of forget-me-not blue. "I..." He pulled her against him again and swooped down on her mouth once more without finishing the thought.

Young Whitby had come a long way in a very short time under her tutelage. His lips covered hers in a commanding way that made her insides go liquid and her pussy throb and ache for fulfillment. After a moment, he abandoned her mouth to kiss her jaw and neck, sucking and licking the exposed flesh.

Meredith tilted her head back to allow him better access to her throat. Her eyes fell closed and she let his strong arms support her melting body. "Ahh. Perhaps... Unh... I should show you to my room now."

Chapter Four

Despite what his father thought, Chris was neither a fool nor particularly naïve. He'd known when he agreed to come to the countess's estate that it was not merely to examine her greenhouse. The kisses at the Botanical Gardens had clarified that.

It had taken him a few days of consideration to decide whether he was ready to accept what she offered, but he was tired of his celibate life, tired of imagining what intimate congress with a woman might be like, tired of holding to some high ideal of intellectualism over base urges that he'd set for himself. Yes, he'd known when he responded to her invitation what he was letting himself in for. Meredith de Chevalier was a sophisticated, experienced woman who took her pleasure whenever and wherever she chose and for some reason she'd chosen him. He was damned well going to take advantage of her tutoring in the art of lovemaking.

What he hadn't counted on was how quickly things would escalate from a few kisses to her taking him by the hand and nearly dragging him upstairs to her bedchamber. Not that he didn't want to go. But his head spun with the heady liquor of lust, or perhaps from the lack of oxygen due to kissing, and he wished he might have a moment to get his bearings before the act began.

There was her bed, the tall posts draped in blue fabric, the white and blue coverlet pulled back invitingly. In a few moments they were going to be lying together on it. He would be inside her body. His cock swelled in anticipation yet at the same time his stomach twisted. What if he didn't do it right? What if he made a fool of himself by exhibiting his virginal inexperience? Oh God, he wished he'd taken his father up on that offer of practicing with a prostitute. He would surely reveal his incompetence, perhaps move too fast or release too soon, or worse, lose his momentum completely.

She turned to him, her eyes bright and a smile playing over her lips. Her black hair had fallen completely loose from its pins due to his hands being plunged into it. She looked charming with the curls framing her heart-shaped face. Her jonquil-colored dress was like a ray of sunshine in the dim room, which was shuttered against the heat of the day. The slats of the shutters were open just enough to let in a faint breeze and a few rays of light that illuminated the elegant furnishings and plush carpet.

"Are you ready?" The countess stroked the side of his face. "You look uncomfortable."

"No. I'm fine. I'm ready." He breathed deeply, trying to calm his racing heart.

Once more she curled her hand around the back of his neck and pulled him down to her as she rose up on the balls of her feet, reminding him of how short she was. "Just kiss me. The rest will follow naturally," she whispered, before blending her lips with his.

He closed his eyes and did as she bid, and of course, she was right. It felt good and natural to hold her in his arms. His hands knew what to do, where to touch, how to stroke up her back and then down again to hold her rear. Her buttocks were buried beneath layers of fabric but he still felt a thrill at the unbelievable liberty of touching them. He pulled her tight against the hard erection filling the front of his breeches. It was nearly painful in its throbbing need. The yielding softness of her body both relieved and made the ache even worse. He needed to be inside her, not rubbing against her.

He kissed her mouth, slipping his tongue between soft lips to touch hers. She teased him, darting her tongue out and pulling it back in a little game that made him smile. He'd never realized playfulness might be a part of lovemaking.

After kissing her softly and gently then hard and deep for several minutes, he pulled his mouth from hers and moved it to her neck. The smooth, warm skin beneath his lips, the pulse of life in her throat and the salty taste of her skin sent new waves of desire coursing through him. He licked down the column of her throat and along her delicate collarbones. Her soft intake of air, such a sweet, feminine sound, made him feel strong, powerful and very masculine.

He dared to dip his mouth lower, to kiss the flat plane of her chest down to the soft swell of her cleavage. The top mounds of her breasts pushed up by her tight bodice were displayed in a tempting froth of lace that framed them like a picture. He kissed them. By God, his mouth was on her breasts and they were so incredibly soft. Their plump fullness yielded to the pressure of his lips. They were scented with rosewater and he thought he would never again smell a rose without thinking of her breasts.

Her hands threaded through his hair, pushing on his head slightly and encouraging his exploration of her breasts. "You may remove my dress," she murmured, tugging on his hair to pull him away.

Chris straightened and the countess turned her back to him that he might unfasten the row of hooks down the back of her bodice. His hands felt huge and clumsy as he concentrated on the painstaking assignment. He was in too much of a hurry and his fingers trembled from nervous excitement. Giving an impatient grunt, he considered ripping the dress open.

"Patience, *ma petite*." She laughed and her smooth white shoulders shook. "Open your present slowly. Savor each moment."

He resumed the task and this time followed her advice, bending to kiss each inch of flesh as it was revealed. She wore no corset beneath her high-waist dress, just a light camisole, the fabric so sheer it revealed her rosy skin. He kissed her right through the cloudy material, his mouth wetting it and molding it to her flesh.

As soon as he had enough hooks unfastened, he peeled the bodice down her body while she pulled her arms from the small, puffed sleeves. He pushed the dress over the flare of her hips and let it fall to the floor in a pool around her feet. Within seconds he had her camisole peeled off, too, and turned her to face him.

Other than white marble statues in a museum, he'd never seen a naked woman. The mystery of the soft mounds a woman's décolletage only teasingly advertised was revealed to his sight. His breath caught as his gaze riveted on the pale globes of flesh, small and high with rosy aureoles and peaked nipples centered in each. They were lovely. He thought he could simply feast on the sight of them for hours, but his body had other ideas. His hands reached for them and his tongue swept over his lips, eager to taste them.

Touching her breasts tenderly, he stroked the flesh, as soft as a kid glove, feeling the texture beneath his fingertips. Then he cupped one in each hand and tested the weight and firmness. Finally he could resist no longer and drew one erect tip into his mouth. He rolled his tongue over it and sucked lightly. Such bliss!

He never stopped to worry if he was doing it right, and the countess moaned softly, assuring him that she was pleased. While his tongue laved the slope of her breast and suckled her nipple, he continued to fondle her other breast, rolling the tip between his thumb and forefinger lightly.

"You can pinch a little. I don't mind."

Chris glanced up to meet her eyes, the dark gray of a stormy sky.

"A little pain mixed with the pleasure is a good thing."
She smiled. "As long as the lady wants it."

He tested the truth of her words, squeezing the erect bud harder and even twisting it a little. She gasped, an extended "ahh" of satisfaction.

Switching sides, he gave equal treatment to her other breast, sucking, licking and nipping until her moans grew louder. The sound of her pleasure undid him. He pulled away from her chest and dragged his shirt over his head, casting it aside. Then he reached for the front of his breeches.

While he stripped, she removed her petticoat and drawers. He was torn between looking down at his underdrawers where a knot in the drawstring was slowing him down, and staring at the rest of her body as it was uncovered. Waist, hips, belly... He swallowed and stared as the patch of dark curls marking her sex was revealed, followed by pale thighs. She bent to take her underwear off her legs and his view was cut off for a moment. Chris fumbled with the knotted drawstring, cursing under his breath.

"Here, let me help." She pushed his hands aside and with her long fingernails picked at the knot holding him captive.

His pulse pounded as he gazed at her nude body standing inches away from his—the breasts, which he'd come to know so well in only a few short minutes, and the secret place between her thighs he had yet to explore.

The countess untied the drawstring and pulled his

pants down. His cock sprang forth, fully erect and bobbing gently in the air like a marionette whose string has been pulled. She quickly helped him shed the rest of his clothes, then took his cock in one hand, encircling its girth in the warmth of her palm and fingers.

Chris couldn't prevent the groan that escaped him at the glorious sensation of her touch. His member was suffused with blood, dark red at the head and already leaking white droplets. As she moved her hand up and down once, twice, three times, he drew in a breath and held it, willing himself not to spill over her massaging fist.

It was nearly impossible to believe this was happening. No hand but his own had ever touched him there. The sheer wonder of that contact alone was enough to put him over the edge. But he gritted his teeth and held out for the wonderful things he knew were still coming.

"You're hungry for it, aren't you?" Her voice was husky and her eyes dark as she gazed into his face. "I shan't make you wait much longer. Not this time. Come now." Releasing his cock from her firm grip, she took his hand and led him toward her bed.

She pulled back the covers and climbed onto the high mattress, then held out her hand for him to join her.

Chris paused only long enough to make a mental picture of how she looked at this moment, reclining on her bed, her skin flushed pink as a rose, her eyes huge in her small face, her black hair tumbling like a cloud around it. Oh how beautiful she was! He would never forget this image as long as he lived, or the thunderous, momentous feeling building inside him. Life as he knew it was about to change from the moment he mounted the bed...and the woman.

He straddled her body, her knees on either side of his hips, his arms braced beside her head. His skin brushed against her silken skin. His cock nestled in the soft nest of hair at the juncture of her thighs. He gazed into her eyes. He was poised and ready, but waiting for a signal to continue. His body trembled as if he had the ague, it was so primed and ready to explode into action.

Her hands slipped down between them and fondled his cock. Chris groaned when she guided it to her moist entrance and placed it there, just inside. His jaw knotted as he fought back the urge to ram into her with a savage thrust.

She gripped his buttocks and pulled him toward her. "It's all right. Come inside me." The invitation was music to his ears. He pushed into the heat and wetness of her body with a protracted sigh. Her inner muscles clenched around him, drawing him deeper, welcoming him inside. "That's good," she whispered. "Just like that."

Her soft encouragement filled him with glowing warmth and spurred him onward. He paused for a moment, seated deeply inside her, enjoying the tremendous heat surrounding him, hotter even than the swelter of the greenhouse, then he withdrew his entire length. Her body surrendered him reluctantly, wet suction holding his shaft tightly as he pulled out.

In again. Another thrust buried him balls deep inside

her. Chris grunted as he came home. "Oh, God," he murmured.

Her feet slid up his calves and her legs cradled his hips before wrapping around his lower back, grappling him to her like climbing ivy. "Again!" she ordered.

He needed no further encouragement for he was already pulling out to thrust once more. The new angle of her body made his penetration even deeper. Her slippery channel surrounded him, easing his way so that he glided as smoothly as a boat cutting across a lake.

His arms quivered from the effort of supporting his weight and he let his body ease down on top of her. She didn't seem to mind but slid her arms around his back and clutched his shoulders from behind. Her head nestled into the crook of his neck and shoulder and she nuzzled him there, kissing, licking then biting his flesh.

With each thrust, he grew more confident, his doubts about his prowess fading away. This was what his body was made for. It felt completely right to fill her like this. He wanted to be lost inside her body, to become one with her, and as his desire mounted to fever pitch, this seemed quite possible. Their very flesh was melded together with sweat and juices.

He stroked faster and harder, hips pumping. She met his every thrust, emitting soft moans and whimpers as she wrapped herself around him. Then, quite suddenly, pleasure burst through him like the moment when a seedling first breaks from the soil and unfurls to the sunlight. It felt like fledgling stars were exploding inside him, suns and moons and an entire cosmos spreading through every fiber of his being. He was electrified and alive in a way he'd never experienced before. A cry burst from his throat and he froze while wave after wave of ecstasy churned through him.

When the last pulse had diminished, he came back to an awareness of his body as an earthbound entity and the knowledge that he and the woman beneath him were indeed two separate beings. His eyelids flickered open and he gazed at her shoulder and a lock of dark hair curling over it. Her fingers, which had been embedded in his shoulders, now stroked soothingly up and down his back.

"Good?" she whispered.

He lifted his face to look into her dark-fringed eyes. "Very good. I didn't know how it would be, that it could be so...powerful."

"I know." She nodded. "But, believe me, it's not always that good. It's not the same with every partner."

"You've had a lot?" The question was inappropriate, but he meant no judgment by it, merely curiosity.

She smiled. "A few. Maybe more than my share."

"Was I, uh, adequate?" There seemed no point in pretense in this intimate, honest moment.

Her smile widened as she caressed his cheek. "You were perfect."

He blushed. Of course she would say that. She was kind and wouldn't tell him if he was utter crap at it. But it felt like the truth. Their bodies had felt good together, hitting a rhythm that seemed to please her as much as it did him. A thought occurred to him. "Did you... I mean, do women achieve the same...level of fulfillment?"

"Do we orgasm? Yes, women can and do, but many men never bother to find that out, I'm sorry to say."

He had a hard time meeting her direct gaze as he asked his next question. "Did you, just now?"

"No. But that's all right. We have plenty of time. It doesn't happen so quickly and easily for women as for men." Her eyes crinkled at the corners as she smiled. "But I'll show you ways to ensure your partner climaxes every time."

His cheeks burned at the forbidden words "orgasm" and "climax" tripping so easily from her tongue. How silly that he could perform the act and still blush to hear it spoken of. But he wanted her to teach him how to make a woman come. He wanted to make the countess cry out in helpless abandon as he had just done and to see her expression when she was lost in ecstasy.

The countess. He could probably call her Meredith now that their relationship was on much less formal footing. How strange it was that he hadn't even said her name out loud yet.

"What are you thinking?" she asked. "I can see thoughts flickering in your eyes."

"Meredith." He tested the sound on his tongue. "I was just wondering if you take some precaution to prevent, ah, pregnancy." He'd read of herbal concoctions. It hadn't occurred to him until just now that he should have used a French letter to encase his penis.

"There's no need. I'm barren," she said simply. "My lack of ability to bear children was one of the problems in my marriage. One of many."

"You were very unhappy with him, weren't you?" Chris rolled to lie by her side, his head propped on one hand.

"Yes. It was a loveless marriage. He was...a cruel man, physically as well as emotionally brutal, and it took me many years after his death to discover that sex could be pleasurable." Her voice was low and even, unemotional despite the tragedy she was describing.

Chris was horrified. He'd never have imagined that someone as vital and self-possessed as the countess had been subjected to such horrors. What kind of man would take the incredible gift of her love and abuse it? He understood such things went on in the world, but had never discussed them with anyone. For her to share her story with him was astonishing, and it was almost more than he wanted to hear.

"I'm so sorry." He rested a hand on her flat stomach, wishing he could do something to erase what had happened.

"It was a long time ago. I've put those days behind me and now I live my life exactly as *I* please, something that sufficient funds allow one to do."

He nodded agreement. If he wasn't dependent on a stipend, he could pursue his dream of traveling. But if he crossed his father and became a professor at Cambridge, he would be cut off and might never have the money needed to travel the world. University grants weren't plentiful. "Money may be the root of all evil, but it certainly is necessary."

She laughed. "It does make life more comfortable." She ran a hand down his sweat-slicked chest toward his groin. "And speaking of comfort, I shall ring for some bath water. Or better, we might walk down to the lake and take a dip, save my poor maids from heavy labor on such a hot day."

"I should like that. I enjoy a swim."

"I believe that." Her hand slid up his arm, feeling his biceps. "How does a bookish professor gain such muscle?"

"Rowing on the lake in the park nearly every day."

"Well, it's built up your arms admirably." Over and around his shoulders and to his chest her hand roamed idly. His cock stirred weakly in response. "My goodness, I had no idea you looked like this beneath your clothes. An Adonis. We must buy you tighter fitting jackets and breeches to show off your assets to greater advantage."

The approval in her voice spurred a warm feeling inside. It was nice to be desired sexually, and not something he'd ever experienced before. While it made him blush, it also pleased him very much.

Her hand trailed down to his groin again and grasped his flaccid penis, stroking it lightly. "I will teach you to dance and to cut a fine figure at a ball. Flirting comes naturally when one is confident in oneself. When I'm finished, you won't be able to enter a room without all female eyes turning toward you."

His elation diminished at her words. "I don't care for any of that. I don't want to go to social events and only attend occasionally when my mother comes close to an apoplectic fit. Dancing and flirting don't interest me."

Her eyebrows rose. "Not at all? My dear, you're never going to find a wife without putting forth at least a little effort."

"I don't want to. I'm perfectly happy in my bachelor life. My work interests me more than listening to the empty-headed chatter of some female...uh, present company excepted, of course."

"Of course." The glimmer of amusement around her mouth let him know she was laughing at him inside. "No women for you."

The irony wasn't lost on him. "Perhaps not 'no women' ever, but whomever I choose would have to be someone very special, someone with whom I could converse and share my thoughts. I don't care to spend the rest of my life discussing whether the Prince Regent might possibly make an appearance at some function or evaluating the merits of various gowns. I would want a woman of substance."

"That's a very tall order. You might have to settle for well bred and biddable. That's what most men seem to do." She rolled to her side and pressed a kiss to his chest, as she continued to tug on his burgeoning erection. "Someone who will, mmm, oversee the house and bother you as little as possible while you pursue your important manly affairs."

His hips lifted toward her touch, and a delicious shiver of lust ran through him from the point where her tongue played with his nipple. When she nipped it between her teeth, he gasped sharply. "Ahh!"

She glanced up, a mischievous twinkle in her eye. "Perhaps we might postpone our swim for a little longer and I could show you one of the techniques I mentioned for bringing a woman to orgasm—with me as the test subject."

"I would love to do whatever I can to please you. You've given me so much." Chris spoke the words with complete sincerity. He suddenly realized, as Meredith switched her attention to his other nipple and bit it just as sharply, that this woman was exactly the perfect woman he'd described. It wasn't only her sensuous nature and sexuality that attracted him to her, but her forthrightness, her intellect and wit and her interest in many subjects. She was perfect, and somehow, miraculously, had entered his life.

Meredith had seen him across a room and recognized qualities in him that attracted her. She'd seen a kindred spirit in him that called to hers. His heart swelled at the idea of it. This was a woman with whom he could actually imagine falling in love. She might just be the one he'd been waiting for all his life.

Chapter Five

Oh no. The puppy dog adoration in Christopher's eyes was not a good sign. The last thing Meredith needed or wanted was the young man under her tutelage to become besotted with her. That wasn't at all what Lord Whitby had in mind when he asked her to take him in hand.

Sex was fine. She enjoyed it in all its varied forms, but love was not something in which she indulged or even believed. It was best to disabuse him of notions of romance right away. "Christopher..."

"Please, call me Chris."

"Yes. Well. I want you to understand before we go any further that this is a pleasant diversion, a dalliance, nothing more. Enjoy yourself, but don't do yourself the disservice of becoming attached to me. There is no future here." She smiled as she said it, trying to take the sting from her words, and her hand never lost its grip on his cock, a sure way to get a man to agree to most anything.

"Oh...no. Of course not." There was a momentary flicker before his blue eyes became calm as a glassy lake. "I'm no sophisticate, but I'm not a child, either. I understand about these kinds of affairs. Naturally there could be nothing besides, um, sexual congress between us."

She nearly laughed at the stilted phrase, but maintained her composure. "Good. I'm glad that's understood."

"Yes." The word was a bit strangled as he gasped from the pressure of her hand around his penis.

"Now, my sweet. Let me give you a little treat and then I'll ask for the same favor in return." She kissed his lips, then slid down the length of his body, kissing his chest, the twitching muscles of his stomach and the tops of his thighs. She nestled her body between his legs and faced his cock, a thick, sturdy length that had already proved more than adequate in fulfilling her. She believed that girth beat out length every time. The delicious stretching of her quim was crucial to her pleasure.

Glancing at his eyes, she made a show of licking her lips and slowly leaning toward the head of his cock, giving him plenty of time to anticipate what she was about to do. His eyes widened and his lips parted as he gave a soft "Oh" of surprise. Bending her head, she took the tip of his penis in her mouth and rolled her tongue over it, tasting the salty musk of semen and sweat.

His eyes nearly closed in pleasure, and he moaned.

Meredith swallowed him deep, then deeper still, taking him in up to the hilt. The fullness of his cock in her mouth was as satisfying as a three-course meal. She longed to bite down, give him a little pain with his delight, but it seemed too soon for that kind of game. She withdrew his length almost completely before sucking it in again. Meanwhile, she worked her hand up and down the base of his shaft and reached between his legs to fondle his balls. Within minutes he was groaning and thrusting, his hands threaded through her hair, gripping her head and holding it steady as he pumped into her mouth.

Knowing Chris had probably never experienced anything like this before was a very satisfying feeling. When her husband had forced her to suck him, Meredith had always felt used and demeaned, but since then she'd learned oral sex could give her a powerful charge. She was the one with the control in her hands and mouth, stimulating a lover and guiding him to orgasm. A man was a helpless slave to the desire she brought forth in him, which was both exhilarating and fulfilling for her.

She stopped when Chris's breath grew harsher and his thrusting more erratic. She didn't choose to have him come yet and pulled her mouth from his cock, releasing his shaft from her encircling hand.

He groaned in disappointment and continued to thrust against air for a beat or two. His eyes opened to look at her questioningly.

"Not yet." She smoothed a hand over his hip and down his thigh. "Hold onto that tension. Feel it, enjoy it, but don't let go yet." Stretching out beside him, she rested a hand on his chest and gazed into his eyes. "How does it feel?"

"Painful!" he answered promptly. "Aching and yearning for more. I've massaged myself to fulfillment before, but this is completely different."

"Now, you do the same for me." Taking his hand, she guided it between her legs. "Touch me here. Feel how wet and open I am for you? With every stroke of your fingers my need grows greater. Go between my legs and see what you're touching, and then I'll show you what you can do for me."

He bit his lip and nodded. He sat and moved to kneel between her widespread legs. His poor, blood-suffused cock stuck out at a sharp angle from his body as he knelt there gazing at her feminine assets. His avid examination aroused her. His eyes were like fingers touching her, making her feel voluptuous and completely sexual. Her already melting pussy felt as if it was opening even wider for him. Meredith lifted her hips in anticipation.

Chris reached to touch her labia with a gentle stroke of his fingers that sent fire sizzling through her. He parted the folds and gazed at the dark entrance they concealed. "It's like a blossom," he marveled. "Petals shielding the reproductive organs of the flower." She imagined how her pussy looked to him, glistening wet, plump and pink, the shadowed darkness of her entrance.

"Here." She touched her finger lightly to her clit, jerking at her own touch. "This is where a woman's passion may be stirred." She took her hand away and he followed her lead, tickling the erect nub with his fingertip.

Meredith moaned quietly and shifted.

A smile curved his lips. He touched her again.

Pleasure radiated from the point of contact, but she

wanted more than this tentative touch.

He tapped the little button several times, then rotated it in small circles.

"Ah, yes," she murmured, wiggling in satisfaction. "Like that."

After he'd manipulated her clit for a short while, he bent to inhale her scent as if her cunt was one of his rare flowers. He hesitated there, several inches away from her, and Meredith raised her hips, offering herself to him. "Please. You may touch me there with your mouth."

Lowering his head slowly, he pressed a close-mouthed kiss to her pussy. Then he extended his tongue and carefully lapped over her clitoris.

Meredith gasped and rolled on the bed. "More!" she begged. Good heavens, she'd had sex with dozens of people in her life thus far, had experienced cunnilingus performed by experts in the art, but this young man's hesitant exploration fired her in ways she'd never imagined. It was his very carefulness and uncertainty that set her blood raging.

His hands rested on her hips, fingers holding her labia spread wide as he nuzzled the crevice between. He licked her seam, then flicked his tongue over her clit, at first lightly, then in steady strokes. More flames seared through her, crackling and spreading out from that point like wildfire. She moaned and bucked beneath him, and in mere moments the fire consumed her. With a harsh cry, she arched off the bed, nearly knocking him from her. But Chris held onto her hips and kept his mouth fixed to her pussy, relentlessly licking and encouraging every last bit of pleasure from her.

"Oh! Enough!" She had to push his head away when the intensity grew too great. "Enough now. Thank you."

He let go of her then and propped himself on his elbows, watching her.

Meredith's eyes opened to meet his intrigued gaze. Her breaths were short and shallow as she recovered from the strong climax and brought herself back under control.

"You achieved fulfillment," he stated the obvious in an awed tone. "Just like that? It was so easy."

She smiled. "Sometimes it takes longer, but yes, if a man knows what he's doing and prepares his paramour appropriately and if her passions are engaged, it can be that simple for a woman to come." She reached for him. "Now come up here and let's finish this."

He crawled up her body, positioned himself at the juncture of her legs and guided his cock inside. A soft sigh escaped him and his eyelids fluttered closed as he buried himself to the hilt.

Meredith considered showing him a new position, flipping them so she was on top or encouraging Chris to take her from behind. But he was already deeply embedded in her, his rhythm mounting so she wrapped her arms and legs around him and cradled him tight as he strove for his climax. How she loved the feel of a man in her arms, the weight and heat of his body, the primitive grunts as his cock pushed and pushed into her as if he wanted to become one with her body.

The remaining sparkles of light inside her gathered and coalesced at a point deep within where the head of his cock stimulated her. She relaxed and allowed herself to rise higher and higher on increasing waves of sensation. The feelings peaked and she hung for a moment, suspended in midair, before plunging down.

At the same time, Chris groaned and froze, shuddering against her. They clung together, separate yet one at that moment of union.

Meredith breathed heavily, her chest compressed by his weight on top of her. She stroked his back and cupped his buttocks, kneading the tight muscles with gentle pressure. The heat in the shuttered room had built along with their passion, and sweat melded their bodies together. It was time for that swim now.

She squirmed a little and Chris rolled to the side, releasing her. He flopped onto his back, blew out a breath and pushed a hand through his hair as he gazed up at the canopy above them. "I shan't be able to move from this spot for at least an hour," he claimed. "I haven't a drop of energy left in me."

"Oh, I think you can." She poked him in the ribs. "Think of cool, refreshing water only a short walk away. We can plunge into my pond without a stitch on. There's no one to see us, and should they catch a glimpse, my servants are discreet."

"You entice me, madame. Very well." He rose from the bed and bent to the floor to pick up his clothes, giving her an entrancing view of the play of muscles in his back and ass and long legs. Such a handsome sight. She was quite sure there would be more sexual play in the beauty of nature by her secluded pond. The man would just have to plumb his depths and find another drop or two of energy to expend on her.

ℰↄ

Chris had never imagined the decadence of having sex outdoors on a soft bed of grass or the erotic thrill of pinning a woman against a broad tree trunk while thrusting into her. He'd never fantasized making love in the murky waters of a pond while fishes tickled his legs and mud squelched between his toes. The cool water, the burning sun on his head, the strong legs wrapped around his hips and the hot pussy holding him tight were sensations he couldn't have dreamed of before the countess entered his life.

The woman was as earthy as a tribal goddess, as ethereal as a spirit. She enthralled and possessed him with her body and her infectious laughter. In one brief day she coaxed him from his chrysalis of circumspection to a full unfurling of his metaphorical wings.

When he woke in her bed the next morning, Chris knew he would never be the same.

He yawned and stretched luxuriously like a wild animal awakening from winter hibernation. His arms and legs sprawled over warm woman flesh, his face slid against tangled hair. How strange it was to awaken lying next to someone.

He opened his eyes, eager to see Meredith's beautiful face again, to catch her in an unguarded moment. Her features were relaxed in sleep, vulnerable, sweet. Her slightly parted lips reminded him of a child's, and the sweep of her lashes across each cheek invited a kiss to make them flutter open.

But he didn't kiss her. Not yet. He continued to study her pale skin, the curve of her neck and shoulder, the rise and fall of her breasts as she inhaled and exhaled. She was a precious creation of nature, more intricate and beautiful by far than any plant.

A slight frown creased her forehead then passed away like a scudding cloud. Her eyes moved behind the shield of their lids. What was she seeing? He wished he could share her dreams and protect her from them when they were unpleasant.

Chris caressed the fullness of her bottom lip with his finger and smiled when her mouth moved soundlessly and her eyelashes fluttered.

Her eyes opened. She blinked, focused on him and returned his smile. "Good morning." Her voice was a frog croak and her smile grew even wider at the ugly sound. "Mm, the pleasures of early morning. You go to bed with a princess and wake with a crone."

He imagined he should say something about her being a queen, not a crone. Didn't women like those kinds of compliments? But he wasn't facile with words, and so he simply leaned to kiss her.

That seemed to make her happy, because she kissed him back, curving a hand around his neck and pulling him closer.

He relaxed into Meredith's soft, cushiony body, softer than the mattress, softer and warmer than anything he could think of. His erect cock swelled even harder, wanting to sink deep and deeper into her softness. His penis might be new to the pleasures of woman, but it had caught on quickly to what reward awaited it between her thighs.

As his cock nudged at her entrance, she broke off the kiss and pushed him away with a hand to his chest. "I must take a moment first."

She rolled off the bed and stood gloriously nude beside it, her hair tumbling down her back. She looked wanton, wild and utterly desirable as she glanced over her shoulder at him with heavy-lidded eyes. "I'll return in a moment."

His gaze riveted on her buttocks, which swayed gently as she walked across the room. He watched until the door of her boudoir closed behind her then sank onto the bed and stared at the canopy of pale blue silk overhead.

His life had taken the most unexpected twist imaginable. He felt like a wild thistle seed that had sprouted in a flowerbed. This wasn't his place. He clearly didn't belong in this beautiful bower, but damned if he wouldn't cling to the soil with every ounce of strength he possessed until someone uprooted him.

While Meredith was gone, he took care of his own morning needs, pissing in the chamber pot and washing up in the basin. By the time she returned, wearing an embroidered floral robe in the style of a Japanese kimono, Chris was back in bed, waiting for her. He lay with his arms behind his head, trying to look casual and relaxed as if he lay in a woman's bed every morning of his life.

"I've rung for breakfast. Hope you like crème brochette and black coffee. The only thing I enjoyed about my years in France was the food."

She sat facing him on the bed, her legs drawn beneath the spreading folds of her colorful robe.

He fingered the silk embroidered feathers of a bird near the hem. "Is this from Japan?"

"Yes. Do you like it?"

Chris nodded. "It's very vibrant—like you." He felt silly offering the compliment, even if it was sincere. He hadn't had enough practice to be comfortable chatting with a woman.

"Thank you. And this"—she swept a hand over his naked torso—"suits you perfectly. You should consider wearing it all the time. I'm sure the style would go over well at society events."

He laughed at her teasing and blushed because he couldn't help it. Having a lovely woman admire his body was brand new for him. He couldn't imagine ever tiring of it.

"Now, you must tell me about yourself as a boy." She pulled the folds of her robe out from under her and arranged herself on her stomach, chin propped on her folded arms. "I can imagine you were the kind of child who studied anthills and floated leaf boats on puddles."

"I was. How did you know?"

"Because I was the kind of girl who wanted to be that kind of boy, but mother wouldn't let me get my clothes dirty." Beneath the light tone, her voice was wistful. "I would have been building forts with rocks and sticks and mud if I had a chance. Instead, I had to spend long hours at the piano or stitching embroidery or painting bone china—indoors. I was like a prisoner, allowed outside only an hour a day, and then merely to stroll the garden paths, never to actually dig in the dirt."

"Then you'll enjoy working in your greenhouse," he promised. "I'll insist you get your hands dirty. There's plenty of work for you to do."

She smiled and her eyes twinkled again. "Sounds perfect. Do you know, I've never once played the piano, painted china or embroidered so much as a handkerchief since I left my mother's house? And I never will."

"Did your parents know about...what you had to put up with in your husband's house? Did you ever write to them and ask for help?" Chris knew it wasn't proper to ask such a personal question, but considering all they'd done together and the fact that he was lying naked in front of her, convention no longer seemed important.

For a moment, he thought she wouldn't answer. The pain that shadowed her features made him wish he hadn't asked.

"I tried," she said. "I wrote letters to my mother asking for advice. Of course, I wasn't explicit about what was happening to me, but the suggestion was there. I told her I was very unhappy and asked to come home for a visit. I told her the marriage had been a terrible mistake. I did everything short of begging for rescue, but her response was what you'd expect. She said I must make the best of my marriage. Women are taught it's a wife's duty to create a happy home. If she can't do that, the fault must be in her."

His heart clenched at the bitterness in her voice. Her words made him think about his own mother, a woman completely caught up in society's expectations. Was she happy? Did she love his father? Did she ever dream of a different life, one in which she could build something useful with stones instead of playing countless hands of whist?

He'd never before thought about women wanting to be other than what they were. Since he'd always had to struggle simply to be left alone to pursue his own interests, he could certainly understand the kind of pressure they suffered.

"I'm sorry your life has been so hard." He reached out to touch her soft forearm where it rested on the bed.

She raised her shoulders and shook her head. "This is simply too deep a discussion for so early in the morning. I must have at least two cups of coffee first and I believe I hear Maddie coming now, so you'd better cover yourself before you make her drop our breakfast tray."

Chris scrambled to get off the covers and beneath them at the same time. He'd only just managed to throw the blanket across his waist when the door opened.

A uniformed serving maid entered, walking slowly with a heavily laden silver tray in her hands.

Meredith pushed herself to a sitting position and smoothed the covers. "You may set that right here, Maddie. Thank you."

Chris felt a flush creeping from his neck up to his face at his half-nude display. But if his bare torso embarrassed the maid, she gave no sign, although her eyes did dart to his chest and back to the tray before she set it on the bed.

"Have a lovely morning, and thank you again." Meredith dismissed her.

"Now, you must try Genevieve's pastry. It is a taste of heaven." She lifted a flaky bun dripping with cream to his mouth, and Chris took a bite.

The confection melted on his tongue like a dollop of pure sugar. Next Meredith pressed a cup of coffee into his hand, explaining that the contrast of the bitter brew with the sweet pastry was a perfect combination.

"I rarely drink tea. Coffee is my vice," she confided as she picked up a strawberry and held it to his lips. He bit into the tangy fruit and swallowed the burst of juice.

"I could get used to being hand-fed by an angel. It's a lovely way to start the day." The compliment slipped more easily from his lips this time, and he didn't feel quite so foolish saying it.

Meredith smiled. "You're very sweet, but just wait until you learn the other ways I can serve you strawberries and cream. They're much more interesting than this."

Chris wasn't quite sure what she meant, although her suggestive tone told him it was something he'd enjoy very much.

As they shared the food, she asked about his childhood again. "You never really answered my question. What was your life like growing up?"

"As an only child, I spent a lot of time alone, but I preferred it that way. I could spend hours out in nature just looking at things." He sipped the strong coffee then set the cup aside on the nightstand. "You don't want to hear about this."

"Yes, I do." A drop of cream lingered on her upper lip and he longed to lean in and lick it clean. "Tell me more."

"As a child, I was left to my own devices to play in the woods on our country estate or read my botany books. It was only when I was older my father realized I was a sore disappointment. At boarding school, I didn't play on any teams. Father tried to interest me in hunting when I was home on holiday, but I couldn't see the point in chasing down a fox just to watch the hounds tear it apart. I don't shoot, play cards or drink. I'm not the son he'd hoped for."

"No. I'm sure he doesn't feel that way."

He smiled. "You're kind, but there's no need to sympathize. I know what my father thinks of me, but I don't need his approval and intend to continue pursuing my own ambition."

"Which is to travel to foreign places and collect samples of the local flora?"

"Precisely." He leaned over and offered Meredith another strawberry dipped in cream.

"But that's enough of my life history for now. I'm sure there are more interesting things to talk about. Or we could stop talking entirely for a while and you could show me exactly how you plan to serve me these berries."

Her seductive smile set a warm glow burning in his groin. "You'll have to move the breakfast tray then."

Chapter Six

"Dancing is a form of communication between men and women," Meredith instructed him as she took his hand in hers. "There's so much more going on than formal movements. What passes between people on the dance floor is a suggestion of what happens in the bedroom."

Her eyes bored into his as she stepped toward him. Although only their hands touched and inches of space separated their bodies, he felt as if she was touching him all over. Her eyes were like fire, sucking all the oxygen from the drawing room as they burned hotter and hotter.

Chris immediately forgot the intricate steps of the quadrille she'd taught him and stood rooted to the spot.

She laughed and pushed his arm. "No. You have to keep moving. But you see what a single glance can do? Now, let's begin again."

She nodded to the fiddle player she'd hired from the village and he started the tune over. Taking Chris's hand, she guided him through the beginning steps of the set—heel, toe, point and turn.

"Why are we doing this?" His hand touched hers,

palm to palm as they rotated in a circle.

"Because, sir, you need to learn how to conduct yourself in the ballroom. Did your dancing master give you any instruction at all?"

"He tried. I wasn't an apt pupil."

Chris had lost count of the number of steps to the right and tried to turn too soon. He bumped into Meredith, breaking the rhythm and stopping the dance once more. He stood stock still as she continued to move gracefully around him.

"This is impossible. How can we practice a dance intended for an entire line of people?"

"If you can remember all of those Latin names for plants, I'm sure you can learn these steps, even practicing with invisible partners. But the most important lesson here is confidence. A woman responds to a man who looks her in the eye as though he'd like to devour her right there on the dance floor."

She looked so luscious in her silver-spangled gown he had a hard time keeping his focus on her face instead of her body. The fabric hugged every curve and her décolletage was so deep her breasts threatened to spill free of the satin. It was easy to imagine devouring that soft, rosy flesh. Chris took a step forward and reached out for her.

"Yes. That's the look. Now if you can only remember to move while doing it," she said.

"I can move." He slipped a hand around her waist and lowered his head to the swell of cleavage. He nuzzled his mouth between the plump mounds without a care for making a spectacle in front of the old violinist. Likely the gaffer had pressed his lips to a woman's breast many times in his life and wouldn't be shocked.

Meredith laughed and pushed his head away. "No distractions. This is a dance lesson. We'll have time for that later."

He heaved a sigh, but straightened.

"I simply don't see the point when I never intend to woo a woman on the dance floor. Balls are never going to be a part of my life."

"One never knows what the future might bring or what skills might be required. Anyway, I've hired this fine musician for the afternoon and I want to dance so please, do me the favor."

She pouted and, like a tail-wagging dog, Chris was eager to please her. "Very well. I'll behave."

Meredith turned to the violinist. "Can you play a waltz, please, Mr. Sanderson?"

"Aye, missus." The liver-spotted hand bowed the string with amazing dexterity considering how swollen the man's knuckles were. Notes trilled like bird song, filling the drawing room where they'd cleared the floor to make a practice space.

"Maybe you'd fare better with the new waltz," Meredith said. "There are fewer steps to remember and it's considerably more intimate than the quadrille or cotillion. Now that it's come into favor, I predict we'll not see much more of the old country dances."

She took his hand and placed it on her waist then raised his other hand and cupped hers around it. "Of course, your partner will be wearing gloves so you must signal your desire with the pressure of your hands alone. The strength of a man's palm at a woman's back, his grip on her hand and a piercing stare are enough to make many a young lady swoon."

"Or maybe it's the ridiculous corsets they wear."

"One-two-three, one-two-three. Do you hear it? No, don't look down at your feet. Look into my eyes. And don't think so hard. Don't count. Just feel the rhythm and move to it."

He glared at her. "Stop shouting instructions at me and I might be able to hear the music."

A quiet chuckle blended with the sweet trill of the fiddle. Chris glanced at the ancient musician. A smile twisted one corner of his mouth and he began to play faster.

Chris fell into step with his partner and found she was right. The waltz was much easier than the quadrille, and it was rather fun, whirling around the room with her in his arms. Her body was so light and responded to his slightest touch, the pressure of his hand letting her know if they were about to glide left or right.

It occurred to him that dancing required quite a bit of trust on the woman's part since she was basically moving backward, blind. If her partner didn't pay attention, he might run his lady into another couple on the floor. Chris felt he did pretty well in guiding Meredith around the cleared space in the center of the drawing room. He didn't trip once although he did kick over a small ottoman that got in the way.

By the time the song was over, both were sweating and winded. Meredith released his hand and pulled away from his embrace to collapse on a divan.

Chris flopped into a chair, legs sprawled in front of him. He blew out a long breath, feeling like a dark horse which had miraculously crossed a finish line.

The fiddler had taken his instrument from beneath his chin and laid it aside. He flexed his arthritic hands and reached for the glass of port on the side table, which Meredith had poured for him.

"You see? Dancing is also very good for the constitution. Doesn't your blood feel afire and full of energy?" She pushed the curling tendrils from her forehead and fanned her face with her hand.

"Absolutely. And I plan to act on that energy just as soon as I can stand again." He gave her a lascivious grin, pleased with himself and his increasing proficiency at flirting.

"A few more dances and I'll take you up on that offer. But first let's have another go at that quadrille."

He groaned and leaned his head back against the chair, closing his eyes. "Infuriating woman. I'm trying to tell you that this is as pointless as teaching a donkey to jig. I will never make use of this lesson."

"Perhaps not." She rose and poured them each a glass of wine from the decanter and handed one to Chris. "But simply knowing you could dance if you wanted to will give you a boost of confidence. Extra confidence is always a good thing."

He shook his head at her logic, and drank deeply of the wine. If it was important to Meredith to teach him to dance, the least he could do was try harder and with less complaining. God knew, she'd done so much for him in just a few days time, turning him from an introverted shadow into a man who could tease and flirt, make love and, apparently, dance.

"All right then. I'll attempt to put my best foot forward instead of tripping on it." He rose and offered her his hand. "Let's dance."

Ⅎℽ

Christopher Whitby was blossoming before her very eyes. Not just from day to day, but minute by minute. She'd taken him in hand only four days ago and what a fine figure of a man he'd already become. A little coaxing was all he'd needed to bring him out of his shell and set him on the path to the full potential of his manhood.

Not that Meredith hadn't found Chris sweetly endearing from the first moment she'd seen him standing amidst his roses. His enthusiasm for his flowers was charming and a refreshing change from the ennui that plagued most society men. But his newfound confidence in his sexual prowess added an undeniable element of charisma. If the ladies of the *ton* and their prissy daughters could see him now, they wouldn't recognize the withdrawn scholar who'd once lurked at the fringes of their card parties, dances and soirées.

He exuded masculine assurance. His mere glance set Meredith burning, his slow smile teased and titillated, the husky timbre of his voice promised pleasures in the bedroom. Perhaps she'd done her job too well. All his father had requested was that she sexually awaken him, priming him to secure a bride. But now he was far too sultry to unleash on those priggish society misses. They wouldn't know what to do with such a man.

Or maybe it was only in her eyes that he was the epitome of a male. As days slipped past, she found herself increasingly enthralled with the young man under her tutelage and had to keep reminding herself their involvement was only temporary.

"Do you like that?" His voice brought her back from her musing to the bed where they reclined, naked, against the pillows. For a moment, she thought he was talking about his hand absently stroking her bare leg.

"Yes." The warmth and weight of his touch made her skin tingle and her nipples harden. Then she realized he was talking about the pen and ink sketch of the greenhouse interior on the paper in front of him. "Oh, yes. Lovely."

She studied the drawing of trees, shrubs and flowers that would bring the abandoned conservatory back to life. A fountain gushed in the center of converging pathways and wicker seats nestled in a grove of palm fronds. She could imagine curling up there, sipping a cup of coffee or dozing in the sun. "Perfect. There's only one thing missing."

"What?"

"A trellis arching over the path. Maybe with wisteria or roses growing on it."

"There's not really room for that." His gaze lifted to her face and his eyes softened in a look of adoration. "But I'll see what I can do."

She kept trying to discourage Christopher's emotions, periodically reminding him that his stay with her couldn't last. But at the same time, she was growing accustomed to the warm look with which he always greeted her. Every time he saw her after a brief absence, his expression was one of epiphany—as if he'd only just discovered a rare and wonderful plant specimen. What woman wouldn't want to be worshipped like that?

But his ardor was only an illusion, lovestruck blindness ignited by a strong dose of lust. It would cool in time. After their affair ended, he'd begin to see their relationship for what it really was—a mutually satisfactory exploration of two healthy bodies. His heart might hurt a little at first, but in hindsight, Chris would thank her for tutoring him and giving him the perfect introduction to sex.

"Your drawing is very good." Meredith studied the finely drawn lines. Cross-hatching added shadow and depth to the clusters of greenery. He'd even managed to convey sunlight streaming in from the glass ceiling. On one of the benches he'd drawn Meredith sitting and reading a book, just as she'd imagined.

She traced a finger over her image, smearing the ink slightly. "Sorry. I thought it was dry."

She examined the ink on the pad of her finger. It appeared black on the paper, but as she smeared it between her thumb and forefinger, she realized it was indigo. It left a purple smear on her skin. An interesting thought occurred to her. "You should draw me now. Not draw me, but draw *on* me—like a native tattoo, but without needles."

Chris paused with the pen poised above the inkpot on the tray beside him. "Draw what?"

"Anything. Tribal markings like primitives decorate themselves with or a mermaid like sailors wear. Whatever you want to create."

"This ink doesn't wash off easily," he warned. "And the pen nib will poke."

"I know. I *want* the drawing to remain for a while, and I want to feel the scratch of your pen on my skin."

"Where?" Ink dripped unnoticed from the pen onto the tray. His eyes were alight with interest, intrigued at the erotic notion of drawing on her flesh.

She turned her back toward him. "An entire canvas for you to design."

He accepted her offer. A few moments later Meredith lay face down on the bed, her head turned sideways on the pillow, her body quivering in anticipation of the first stroke of his pen.

Chris sat beside her, his warm palm and fingers splayed across her back. He rubbed his hand up and down her back lightly as though learning the texture of her skin. "You're sure about this?"

"Yes." Her tongue darted over her lips. She pressed her throbbing sex into the bedcovers, trying to ease the pressure between her legs.

"I'll do it here, so it will be covered no matter how low the neckline of your gown." His thumbnail traced a pattern on her lower back from the curve of her buttocks up to just short of her shoulder blades.

She wiggled at the tickling sensation. "What will you draw?"

He didn't answer at first, but continued to scratch a design onto her skin with his nail. "Something rare and exotic to represent you."

Meredith smiled. "You really are getting glib with your compliments."

"It's not glib when they're sincere," he answered.

There was another pause. His hand lifted from her back, leaving it naked once more.

She watched as he lifted the ink and pen from the nightstand then she closed her eyes and waited while he shifted closer to her body. She concentrated on the sounds around her: the creak of the bed, his breathing, the clink of metal against glass as the pen clicked against the inkwell.

Holding her breath, she waited for that first scratch, but even though she was expecting it, she started when the nib touched her skin.

"Don't move unless you want a blot," he ordered.

He moved the pen assuredly in a single line that followed her spine an inch to the left then curved sharply over the right side of her back. She tried to imagine what it looked like—a black line on peach skin. He drew another line, parallel with the first, but curving the opposite direction.

She shifted. Her breasts ached, not from being pressed into the mattress, but with the need to be touched. She wished he were drawing on the front of her body.

Chris stopped immediately. "Does it hurt?"

"No. It feels delicious. Keep going."

Another stroke, and another, curving left and right, swirling in spirals and short, straight lines that covered her back. She stopped trying to guess what he was depicting and relaxed into the experience. The end result would be a surprise.

He pressed harder, less cautious now as he immersed himself in the work. Some strokes were quite hard, almost painful; others were featherlight. Her skin was energized and tingled all over. Her pulse throbbed between her legs and she wished he would pause to touch it, but Chris was intent on his artwork, scratching and scratching hundreds of intricate lines.

The room was quiet but for the ticking of the mantel

clock and the minute sounds of Christopher's movements. Meredith fell into a near trance, completely relaxed yet very aware of every part of her body the pen touched. She liked him marking her as if putting his seal upon her and wished it were a real tattoo that would last long after they parted. One day, years from now, she might see him at some social event with his wife, a paragon who'd produced the perfect Whitby heir. Meredith would smile at the woman and think about the design on her back that forever connected her to Chris.

"There."

Her eyes snapped open at the soft word. "Finished?"

"Lie for a few more minutes while it dries." He bent to blow a warm breath over her back.

She made a small sound in her throat and wiggled.

Chris gathered up the sheaf of drawings of the greenhouse design and other renderings of specific plants and fanned her back with the pages.

The cool air made her shift and moan again. "I can't wait to see it."

"And I can't wait to touch you. I'm so hard for you it hurts."

She grinned and looked up at him. "Really? You liked drawing on me."

In answer, he leaned over her and pressed kisses to her upper back from one shoulder blade to the other. His hand slid up the inside of her leg, caressing her thigh then seeking the warmth of her cunt. His fingers eased inside, probing gently and finding her soaking wet.

Coating them with her juices, he reached along her seam until he came to her erect bud.

Meredith lifted her hips off the mattress so he could reach it better.

"You look so beautiful like this," he murmured against her back.

"You like fucking me from behind?"

"I love making love to you in any possible way you can imagine." He straightened and abandoned her pussy, making her whimper in disappointment. He pressed his fingertips lightly to the ink on her back.

"I think it's dry enough now. Although I can't vouch for what will happen to your clothes over the next few days. When you perspire, the ink is bound to bleed onto the fabric." He rose from the bed and held out his hand to her.

"Loss of a few dresses is a small price for pleasure." She took his hand and he pulled her to her feet.

Together they walked to the full-length looking glass. Meredith took up a hand mirror from the top of her bureau and stood with her back to the long mirror, while angling the smaller one to get a better view of her backside.

She drew in a breath. "It's beautiful!"

She studied the tree spreading across her back. The ends of her hair brushed against its topmost branches, the roots reached over the curve of her bottom. The branches coiled in a stylized fashion and an abundance of leaves, fruit and flowers blossomed on each one.

"It's meant to be the Tree of Knowledge in the Garden of Eden."

"Forbidden," she murmured, reaching her hand around her side to touch one of the blooming branches.

"Special and worth any risk. I imagine the fruit was so sweet, so astonishing that neither Adam nor Eve ever regretted tasting it."

"But it brought suffering to them and all mankind."

"So the story goes, but I don't believe it." He came up beside her, his body framing hers in their reflection. His hand snaked around her waist to finger the roots of the tree where they ended on the slope of her buttocks. "I think they enjoyed their new knowledge and lived happily ever after with God's blessing."

She laughed and looked from her ass to his eyes gazing into hers in the mirror. "You, my friend, are an optimist and a romantic."

He grinned. "What can I say? I believe in a forgiving and benevolent God. No wrathful, judgmental Jehovah could create such a beautiful world."

Dropping the small mirror on the carpet, she turned to Chris and wrapped her hand around the back of his neck, pulling him down to her for a light kiss.

"I like your God. Maybe if I'd experienced more of him I'd still attend church," she said. "But, you're right. We should enjoy everything nature has to offer and right now that's..." She broke off and rose up on her toes to cover his mouth with hers.

His tongue teased her lips open then snuck inside

where it coiled around hers. The sinuous glide of warmth and wetness awakened a renewed wave of desire in Meredith's belly. Her body felt pliant and melting as she leaned into his hard muscles. His strong arms held her tight and his hands roamed up and down her back.

She wanted to see what that looked like, his hands stroking over the Tree of Life, so she ended the kiss and cast a glance over her shoulder at the mirror.

They looked beautiful together. Her body was pale and his a shade darker. Her ebony hair tumbled down her back and over his hands. His fingers were splayed wide and beneath them the etched lines of the drawing were dramatic against her white skin. One of his hands slipped down to clutch her ass and the sight of it was nearly as erotic as the feel of those strong, demanding fingers.

His breath blew against her hair and his glowing eyes studied their reflection, too. "You're beautiful." The low murmur of his voice vibrated from his chest into her breasts, which were mashed flat against him.

He kissed her hair then cupped her face and turned it back to him so he could kiss her. He pressed soft little pecks to the corners of her lips, her cheeks, nose, forehead and eyelids. Moving down to her jaw and throat, he licked and tasted her. He pushed the mass of her hair aside and nuzzled her shoulder.

She watched his face while he kissed her. His eyes were closed and the fringe of eyelashes across his cheekbones made her heart catch. He was so pretty. His mouth drifted across her chest and down to her breasts, suckling at one then the other. The tugging in her nipples sent a sharp ache down to her pussy. She sighed and petted his soft hair, letting it sift through her fingers.

Chris moved lower. He kissed the undersides of her breasts then knelt before her as he kissed his way down her belly. Gripping her hips, he brushed his cheek against the neatly trimmed hair at the junction of her legs. He blew a breath through the curls, ruffling them and tickling her clitoris.

She pushed her hips forward, seeking more than that taste of pleasure. Parting the folds of her sex, he ran a teasing finger along her seam, making her shiver.

Meredith watched their reflection in the mirror as Chris leaned forward and kissed where his finger had touched. She loved the sight of him concentrating so intently on her intimate parts. And she liked the way she looked as he touched her there, her body yearning toward him and her eyes falling half closed. The eroticism of watching combined with the feel of his stroking tongue and fingers.

She arched toward him again, wanting even more. Her pussy yawned and ached to be filled.

As he continued to swirl his tongue around and over her clit, he slipped a finger inside her, then a second. A third. He drove them in and out and her muscles clenched around them, trying to pull them deeper.

His relentless tongue lapping at her clit brought her closer to the edge of orgasm. She moaned and grasped his head between her hands, thrusting toward his mouth.

Oh, how sensual the pair of them looked in the mirror with the late afternoon sunlight from the window gilding them bronze. They shone like some erotic statue crafted by the follower of a pagan fertility goddess.

Meredith let her head fall back. The long column of her throat was exposed and vulnerable. Her hair was tangled and wild, and her body thrust wantonly toward her lover's mouth and hands.

When he'd brought her to the very brink of climax, Chris stopped. He rose to his feet and grasped her buttocks, lifting her. Meredith wrapped her legs around him as he positioned her above his cock and slowly pushed inside.

He turned them so that her back was to the mirror. She guessed he was looking at his drawing on her back as he fucked her. She knew it when he whispered hoarsely, "You look so exotic, so beautiful. I can't have enough of just looking at you."

Smiling, she rested her head on his shoulder and held onto his broad shoulders while he moved inside her. She clenched around his shaft, holding him hard and letting go by increments as he slowly pulled out again. Once more he pressed deep and then deeper, pausing inside her without moving. She felt his cock pulsing—a throbbing, living piece of him that was part of her for a few brief seconds.

He let out a harsh breath and pulled back out. Then in, gliding on a slick of juices. Out...and in again. His slow movement grew faster. He rammed harder, grunting softly with every thrust.

Meredith held on tight and bore down as best she could with nothing supporting her besides his arms. His biceps bulged with the effort of holding her. He could have carried her to the bed, but continued to stand before the mirror, watching their lovemaking through heavy-lidded eyes.

She looked back over her shoulder, wanting to see what he saw. The image was startling. His legs were braced shoulder-width apart on the floor, calves trembling from the effort of supporting both their weight. His hands gripped her ass as he thrust into her. She looked delicate and feminine in his powerful arms. Her buttocks and legs tensed and the design on her back ebbed and flowed with her flexing muscles. Sweat glistened on their skin, and both their faces were drawn into frowns of concentration.

She turned her head into his shoulder again, opening her mouth to taste his salty skin, breathing in his animal scent. His cock filled her over and over, stretching and rubbing the lips of her vagina and hitting a spot deep within that made her gasp. Tendrils of desire coiled inside her like elusive wisps of smoke. The smoke thickened, coalesced, grew solid, it filled her and flooded her until she became one with the pleasure. Her orgasm wasn't violent and vibrant, but subtle and profound. She shuddered against Chris as the waves swept through her. Her hands slipped on his sweaty shoulders and she renewed her grip, digging in with her nails.

He gave a small grunt of approval and increased his pace, ramming his cock deep and hard into her creaming pussy. The bliss of her climax was still vibrating through her when he came, too. His groan reverberated near her ear and his body froze. Inside, his cock pulsed and released in steady bursts.

Meredith clung to him even tighter, her ankles clasped behind his back, her torso pressed against him and her arms twined around his neck. Her breath came and went in uneven gasps. His did, too.

He finally broke from his stance before the looking glass and staggered with her over to the bed. Together they collapsed upon it in a tangle of limbs and sated bodies. Her hair was somehow trapped beneath his arm, pulling her head back awkwardly. He rolled them over so he was on the bottom without breaking their union.

For a long moment, they lay simply breathing and recovering their strength. Then her eyes opened, focused and looked deeply into his.

"Thank you for my drawing. I'll never wash my back again." She laughed.

He touched the tip of her nose with his finger. "No. I'll scrub it clean for you, as many baths as it takes. And then you'll be a fresh page for me to draw on again." He smiled and pressed a kiss where his finger had been before adding, "You'll let me stay with you a long time simply to satisfy your curiosity about what I'll draw next."

She felt a sharp twist like a shard of glass ripping her heart at the reminder of an end to their affair—an end that she would bring about of her free will because this relationship was never meant to last.

"Design my greenhouse and then we'll see," was her non-committal reply.

Chapter Seven

Chris measured the spot where he intended to add another transplant bed in the greenhouse. Designing the space was tricky. Trays of seedlings needed room, but weren't particularly attractive. Thus they were contained in a small area while the rest of the conservatory would be given over to fully mature plants and decorative touches like the fountain, benches and a preposterous trellis arch that Meredith insisted on having even though there clearly wasn't enough room for it. The woman could be stubborn, although he had to admit for the most part she'd been very amenable to whatever he suggested.

He was as excited as a child at Christmas about the entire project. To be given a free hand and apparently limitless money to spend on whatever plants, flowers, shrubs and trees he chose was a dream come true. As a scientist, his desire was to choose exotic plants he'd like to study, but the design of the room must be attractive for a layperson as well. He felt he'd struck a nice balance in choosing plants that interested him and would please Meredith. If only she'd drop the idea of the trellis arch! It made no sense in the scheme of things, but she was so attached to it.

"Because it's pretty!" she'd argued with him. "That's why. I must have it."

And so the space he had for the nursery was cut down even further. What he really needed was a separate greenhouse for the seedlings, one where he could control conditions more easily and give the plants exactly what they needed. He paused, wondering if Meredith would consider building an addition.

The sound of the door opening broke him from his reverie in which he'd imagined an entire complex of greenhouses at his disposal. He turned toward the fetching sight of Meredith in a white smock over a lilac gown approaching him.

"Another shipment has arrived." Her cheeks were pink and her eyes bright. She looked nearly as excited as he felt. "Big crates. It must be the saplings. I've told the deliverymen to bring the wagon around the side of the house. There's quite a cutting breeze today and we wouldn't want to freeze our precious babies."

Chris smiled. She was learning quickly about the proper care of all kinds of plants. Understanding that plants, like people, often didn't respond well to change, was an important point in nurturing them. Once an environment was established, the less disturbance the better.

"Wonderful. I've got the earth ready." He'd tilled plenty of composted manure and peat into the soil in preparation for the areca palms he intended to plant. Now it was merely a matter of digging a deep hole for the root ball and watering assiduously until the *Chrysalidocarpus lutescens* acclimated to their new home.

"The ground is christened and everything," Meredith agreed.

A flash of heat stabbed him, and he grinned as he recalled just how they'd baptized that particular plot in the south corner of the conservatory. He'd been digging, churning the soil and mixing it with compost for hours. His arms and back ached and sweat had slicked his naked torso. His hair had been as wet as if he'd soaked his head in a rain barrel, and he was just leaning on the shovel regarding the dark, rich patch of earth when Meredith had arrived with a cool drink of lemonade. He'd drained it in several long gulps.

"It looks very...dirty," she'd remarked, gazing at the ground, "and so do you."

Her hands slipped and slid over his sweaty, filthy chest and stomach, then went for his breeches, unfastening and pulling them down with expert haste. In moments, they'd both been naked and Meredith had grabbed his hand and dragged him down into the soil he'd spent all afternoon painstakingly preparing.

"We can't lie here. I've only just got it aerated. We don't want to compact the earth."

"I do." She hooked her hand around his neck and pulled him to her for a long, deep kiss. "I want to roll around like an animal. Rowr!" Her buoyancy was contagious. Besides, how could one argue with a beautiful naked woman requesting sex?

Over the past weeks the countess had taught him many things about intercourse. He'd never known one could engage in so many positions in so many places. Each nuance of location and pose added a unique flavor to the act, making it fresh every time. He'd found new spots to nibble and kiss on her body, learned what drove her wild and that it might be different things on different days. He'd also learned what incredible pleasure she could give him and that her sweet smile and teasing voice affected him in ways he'd never imagined.

Meredith knelt on her hands and knees and glanced at him over her shoulder. "Just like an animal," she breathed. "Do it."

With no more foreplay than that, no nipple sucking or cunnilingus, Chris had obligingly moved in behind her raised ass and guided his erection to her pussy. She wiggled her bottom invitingly. The white cheeks were soft and supple beneath his gripping hands. He'd grabbed her hips tight and drove into her with a powerful thrust, impaling her deeply.

Meredith had moaned and pushed back against him. "Harder. As rough as you can. I want it like that."

And as he'd continued to slam into her, grunting like a beast, she'd exhorted him to greater efforts using curse words he'd never heard. Raw, animal passions swept through him as he pushed deeper and harder, driving her hands and knees into the soil. The scent of peat and compost had risen in an earthy cloud around them and filled his senses as he came with a tremendous burst that tore a primal cry from him.

Meredith had wailed in response, a cry of release that resounded in the enclosed room, bouncing off the glass walls and ceiling.

When the last wave of climax had faded away, he'd pulled out from between her thighs, and she'd dropped down from all fours and rolled onto her back, her body white against the dark earth. She'd stared up at him, breasts heaving, mouth open, eyes wide. "Now our trees will grow well. The ground is energized and full of life here. And in the future, every time I look at the palms, I'll remember this day."

Recalling the christening made his cock rise in his breeches. It seemed he spent most of the time hard these days. Just the sight of Meredith, a whiff of her perfume or a blink of her long-lashed eyes was enough to set him off. She had him in thrall to her sexual charms...to all her charms, and he was content to be so for as long as she wanted him there.

The dray wagon pulled into sight with a creaking of axles and stopped. Chris pressed a quick kiss to his lover's lips. "I'd better supervise the unloading."

The trees he'd chosen would grow no higher than fifteen feet. Several of the dwarf palms would make an attractive cluster of smooth pale trunks with large, shiny green leaves, providing they survived the move from the greenhouse where they'd been raised. A long ride over bumpy roads while enclosed in crates in weather that had turned suddenly cool was not the best guarantee for survival.

Chris had the draymen carry the crates in, and Meredith dismissed the men with a generous tip in hand. He eagerly opened the crates with a crowbar to reveal the young palms inside.

"More digging," Meredith commented. "That's good. I love to watch you do it."

"Well, you might try lending a hand rather than simply standing around. There are bulbs you could be planting," he reminded her.

"And I intend to." She indicated her pristine white smock. "See, I've dressed for work."

He smiled. "That's hardly a gardener's apron. Aren't you afraid of getting it dirty?"

"Not at all. You just show me how deep you want the bulbs planted and I'll do that while you put in the trees."

After handing her a trowel, he showed her the spot of ground where the flowers would grow. Rather than common varieties of daffodils, hyacinths or gladiolus, he'd chosen more exotic species: a Peruvian daffodil, *Hymenocallis narcissiflora* and a checkered lily, *Fritillaria meleagris*, among others. Each bulb or tuber had certain requirements, and he didn't quite trust Meredith to be too particular about depth—or even making sure the proper end was pointing up. But he had to release his tendency to over-supervise and allow her freedom. It was her garden, after all.

Soon she was kneeling and plugging the bulbs into

the loosened soil, her skirt pooled around her and tendrils of her hair falling around her face. She didn't even notice when he left her for the task of digging holes for the new trees.

As they channeled their efforts into work, the heat and humidity in the greenhouse grew. Chris removed his shirt and considered taking off his undershirt as well. There was no formality or propriety here in Meredith's country cottage. The two of them were beyond the rules of polite society in a world of their own creation. But if he was half-naked, she'd soon have him all naked and the job wouldn't get finished. Chris kept his undershirt on.

He pushed the shovel into the dirt with his boot and removed another heavy load. Judging the hole deep enough, he lifted one of the palm trees, removed the burlap from the balled roots and set it in the ground. As he filled the hole, a voice came from behind him. "You do realize it's crooked."

He tamped the dirt down with his foot and stepped back from the palm, which did indeed tilt slightly to the left. "No it isn't."

"Come now. We can't have a grove of crooked trees. Imagine how unsightly that would be." She folded her arms over her chest as she regarded the planting. A smudge of dirt ran from her forehead all the way down to her jaw. He wanted to lean close and lick her face clean.

"Trees reach for the light. They straighten as they grow."

"Ah, then you admit this one is planted crooked."

He seized her around the waist and pulled her to him, growling, "I admit no such thing." He nuzzled into the side of her neck, kissing her, licking the salt from her skin, tugging on her earlobe with his teeth.

Pulling back, he looked at the tree again. "At any rate, it's too hot to argue. Wait until I have them all planted before you start critiquing. And then, when I have set everything to your satisfaction, we'll go for a swim."

"Mm. I do love to swim." Her voice was a sexual purr intended to remind him of other days they'd spent at the lake, splashing in the water, sunning their nude bodies on the soft grass and making love repeatedly in the shade of a thick canopy of leaves.

"Back to work then." He thrust her away from his growing erection. "The sooner we finish, the sooner we may begin."

Less than an hour later they finished their greenhouse work. Chris watered the new saplings one last time, and together they stood back to admire the effect of the fledgling grove.

"I can imagine them touching the ceiling. They will be stunning," Meredith said. "And to be able to sit on a bench in this paradise in the dead of winter will be wonderful."

"The glazier has replaced the broken glass, but we should have all of the panes examined, the caulking re-sealed and the frame checked before snow flies. A buildup of ice could be disastrous on a weak structure." He shuddered at the image of a glass roof collapsing under the weight of ice to shatter on a vulnerable woman sitting in her garden below. Chris gripped her hand tightly, assuring himself of her safety.

"Ach, we're as grimy as street urchins." She lifted their joined hands. Even though she'd worn gloves, her hands were nearly as dirty as his. "Time for a swim and a hot bath afterward to wash away the smell of pond water."

When they left the warm confines of the conservatory, a fresh breeze brushed overheated skin, evaporating the sweat of their labors and cooling them. "Early for it to be so cool," Chris remarked.

"Not so early. It's September. We shall have to return to London soon."

"Why?" He released her hand and slipped his around her waist. "Neither of us is interested in that social whirl, balls, concerts, parties, gaming. The city isn't where I want to be."

"Perhaps I miss it." She glanced at him with a raised eyebrow. "Don't presume to speak for me. Maybe I like the gaiety of a dance now and then or a shopping trip someplace where I may buy frivolous things. Maybe there are friends I want to see, other people besides you with whom I want to spend time."

Meredith had reminded him periodically during their time together that their affair was temporary. But the deeper his feelings for her became, the more impossible it seemed that she didn't feel the same way about him.

He neither argued nor conceded her point, but shifted to a different angle. "The breeze is nice today. Fresh air is one very good reason to stay in the country. I don't think I can bear the pall of coal smoke every day. It's a wonder everyone in London doesn't have lung disorders."

The path turned around a copse of trees and Meredith pulled away from him to trot swiftly ahead toward the water. She unbuttoned her dress as she ran and had stripped to her underwear by the time she reached the water. She pulled the pins and ribbons from her hair and shook her head, letting the midnight locks tumble around her shoulders.

Chris held back for a moment just to watch her. The erotic sight of Meredith in a corset, stockings and lilac-satin shoes that matched her discarded dress was entrancing. The corset framed her already taut figure, cinching her waist and pushing her breasts up so that they rose in two pale mounds above the top. She wore a garter belt and lacy garters which attached to her sheer white stockings, but her bottom was bare, the pink cheeks thrust provocatively out when she turned and bent toward the water.

After dipping her hand in, she turned and called, "Still warm. The air hasn't cooled it too much yet."

God, her front was even more stunning than the back. In addition to the swell of her décolletage, her dark-haired pussy was on display. He could see a flash of her labia below the concealing thatch and longed to kneel at her feet and explore it further—as if he didn't know every inch of her intimately by now.

"Unlace me," she demanded, turning her back to him.

"Don't know why I ever wear this silly thing when I'm in the country."

He walked up behind her and untied the satin ribbons that held the whalebone corset closed. Eyelet by eyelet, he loosened the ties until she was free and could remove the encasing garment. Her breasts swayed as she tossed it aside, so beautiful, round and soft. The nipples tightened to hard beads almost instantly at the cool kiss of air. His mouth opened in anticipation of sucking one into his mouth. Knowing what her breasts felt and tasted like only made him desire them more all the time. He felt he would never tire of her body or of spending time with this vivacious woman.

His drawing on her back had faded and washed away from repeated swimming and bathing, but he could still see a faint, smeary trace of the Tree of Life. He'd have to decorate her again, perhaps with a rare orchid this time. Gazing at the flexing muscles of her back, he pictured it there. Perhaps he could add color this time and tease her with a paintbrush's tickling stroke.

She unfastened a garter and began rolling down a stocking, then paused to look up at him. "What are you waiting for?"

"Just enjoying the view." He reached for the buttons on the front of his shirt. In moments he'd caught up with her and was as naked as Adam in the Garden. This wild, bohemian lifestyle suited him. He'd never imagined he could shake off his stuffy notion of what a man should be so easily. The high ideals he'd held about the nature of man as an intellectual being set apart from other animals seemed narrow-minded now. He hadn't taken into account that humans have both primitive and divine attributes and both parts are necessary to make a man whole.

By the time he ran into the water, mud squelching between his toes, Meredith was already swimming out to the center of the pond. She turned and paddled in place, watching him come toward her. Her wet hair floated around her shoulders and strands clung to the sides of her face. "A bit chilly today."

He could see from her breasts, bobbing like buoys on the surface of the water, that it was. Her aureoles were puckered and her nipples hard as pebbles. On either side, her arms waved, keeping her afloat, as she reclined back into the water.

Chris passed the point where he could touch bottom and swam to her. He side-stroked in a slow circle around his enchanting mermaid. "You'd leave all this beauty and the freedom to do exactly as you please to return to city life?"

"Maybe exactly what I please is a short sojourn in London. Enough, Christopher! I don't wish to discuss this anymore." Her tone was sharper than he'd ever heard it. "We've had a lovely time. But we always knew it would have to end eventually."

He knew nothing of the kind, and would continue living with her indefinitely if she would agree to it. "You're already tired of me, Meredith? Don't you feel something growing between us—something that might be love?"

She frowned. "Oh please, professor. You have a logical mind. You can't believe in such a romantic notion. Lust. Sexuality. Pleasure in one another's company. Two bodies coming together for mutual satisfaction. Those things are true, but everlasting love is a fantasy."

Chris could actually see her face shutting down, like a flower open to the sun by day, but closing its petals at night. More argument was not going to win his case. He needed to reach her another way, and he must find it, before she ended their affair and whisked them both off to London.

To dispel the tension between them, he swam close to her and slipped his arms around her, drawing her cool, wet body against his. Beneath the surface of the water, their legs kicked gently to keep afloat. He bent to kiss her. Her lips were warm and tasted of pond water. The appeal of the woman in his arms was beyond anything he'd ever imagined.

Chris had idealized women before beginning this passionate affair and learning the truth about the nature of a woman. Hidden beneath layers of garments and shields of propriety, females had seemed like perfect, untouchable beings. Now he knew they sweated, belched, passed wind and secreted sexual juices just like men. They seemed much more approachable, more vulnerable and more endearing. Or perhaps the last just applied to Meredith. He accepted her imperfections and foibles as well as her strengths. He wanted all of her, always—and this after spending only a few weeks together.

A short-lived affair wasn't nearly enough. He had to

convince her to continue their relationship. He had to have her for the rest of his life.

Chapter Eight

She wasn't in love with him, Meredith told herself.

Chris might be a better lover than many she'd had, which was an unexpected development, but he was still just a lover, a temporary diversion to enjoy then discard.

Even if she believed in such twaddle as "love", she would never marry him. She'd be a fool to give up her hard-earned freedom to become a man's chattel—all her properties, her businesses, her estate, her very person legally belonging to him. She'd suffered that once and would never again. No matter how sweet and caring Christopher might seem, he was still a man with a man's tendency to dominate and possess. Well, she would not be dominated or possessed ever again in her life.

Relaxing into the tepid bathwater, Meredith soaped her body. Her maid, Cecile poured warm water over her, rinsing her clean. The heat was comforting and relaxing. Her jangled nerves began to settle and her mind to quiet. There was no need to be in such an uproar over this. A few more days of pleasure with the young man and then she'd follow through on her part of the agreement with Lord Whitby. She'd take Christopher to London and launch him into society with the new confidence she'd engendered in him, not to mention his improved skills in dancing and drawing room conversation.

"I'll wear my rose and cream gown for dinner," she informed her maid. Cecile had been with her a long time and served as more than a dresser or hair stylist. She was the closest the countess had to a confidante, although they never really talked. She was quiet, calm and never showed shock at any of Meredith's antics—no matter whom the maid might happen to catch in her bed of a morning.

Meredith rose, dripping, from the bath and accepted the towel Cecile wrapped around her.

"He's a very personable, soft-spoken and agreeable young man," Meredith said. "And I never knew I should come to enjoy gardening so much. The project began as an excuse to draw him nearer and now it's become very dear to my heart. I shall enjoy my little conservatory in the years to come, watching the plants grow and bloom."

"Yes, madame." Cecile offered her slippers for her damp feet, but Meredith waved them away and padded barefoot to her bureau. She opened the jewelry case, which sat on top, and examined her choices.

"It's not as if I've led him on. I was very clear from the beginning that this was a temporary arrangement. I can't help it that a foolish young man might imagine I'm his true love just because I initiated him sexually."

"Yes, madame." Crossing to the wardrobe, Cecile removed the chosen dress and carried it to the bed where she laid it out. She then gathered Meredith's necessary undergarments from various drawers.

"I know what you're thinking and you're wrong. I haven't changed nor have my feelings about men changed. They serve a purpose in my life, yes. I won't deny that. But I can exist quite nicely either with or without them."

"Certainly, madame."

"One is much like another, all replaceable. And I'm quite content just as I am."

Cecile remained silent.

"I am!" She paused with a pink ruby necklace trailing from her fingers and whirled toward her maid. "After young Whitby has returned to London and found a wife to please his parents, I shall carry on exactly as before. I have my work and my play, my business and my lovers. I don't require anything else."

"No, madame." Cecile held up a stocking in each hand and offered them to her with a gaze as flat and emotionless as stone.

"Oh, do be quiet! I resent your censure. You forget your place." She snatched the stockings and marched over to the bed to sit and draw them on.

"Yes, madame." Picking up a fine, lawn petticoat, Cecile shook out the wrinkles and carried it to her.

Meredith stepped into the circle of fabric, then turned so her maid could tie it at her waist. "Do you believe in love, Cecile?"

"I couldn't say, madame." She drew the drawstring tight.

"Only the very young and the very foolish believe in love," she announced as she raised her arms so Cecile could slip her dress over her head.

"Yes, madame."

ଜ

After dinner that evening, Meredith and Chris withdrew to the parlor, each with a book to read in front of the crackling fire that had been built to take the chill from the air.

They read in companionable silence for a bit, before Meredith's attention drifted from the written words before her. She gazed at the fire for a few moments, enjoying the fluid, shifting colors—orange, yellow, gold and even occasional flashes of blue or green. The qualities of fire were an intriguing dichotomy, always changing yet ever the same. No two fires were exactly alike, but all generated heat and would burn a person who got too close. There seemed to be some deep meaning in that, but Meredith was too warm and comfortable to figure out what it was.

"What are you thinking?" Chris's voice broke her reverie.

She looked over at him. His book, a treatise on botany, lay closed on his lap with his finger marking his place. "Oh, nothing much." She indicated her own book. "I was thinking about the passage I just read. Would you like to hear it?"

He nodded.

"You'd be surprised," she added with a smile. "Books about people can be nearly as interesting as books about plant life."

She began to read. "The dairymaid lifted the hem of her gown until her dimpled knees were revealed and then each milky thigh. 'Like this? Is this what you wanted to see, sir?'

"'That is exactly what I wanted to see, my sweet, and more.' The baron came closer and caressed her rosy cheek with the back of his hand. 'If you trust me, I will show you such delights you never dreamed of.' He stooped and his hand stole beneath the hem of her gown, pushing the bunched fabric even higher. He touched the plump, sweet petals of her sex, stroking them slowly and teasingly until she shivered like a nervous mare.

"'Oh, my. What are you doing to me? I've never felt anything like this before.'

"He highly doubted her words. The wench was flirtatious and smirking rather than shrinking or shrieking. With a smile, he probed his finger gently into the intimate recesses of her nubile young body."

Meredith paused to glance at her audience of one.

Christopher's book had slipped, forgotten, down the side of the chair. He leaned forward, his eyes wide and fixed on her. "That is truly what the book contains?

Writing like that? I never knew there were such books."

"This is only the beginning, my dear. Listen." She flipped to her favorite scene much farther along in the book.

"'Oh please, sir, let me go.' The minx writhed in glorious nudity on his big bed. She struggled against the ties binding her to the four posts. For a moment, the baron was nearly overcome with the desire to leap on her provocative body and possess it. But he maintained his composure and simply watched her squirm for countless moments.

"Such a beautiful sight she was with her thrusting breasts, nipples as hard and red as rubies, her parted legs revealing all to him. Oh, the glistening moisture of her cunny, the delicate lips and the arousing aroma that rose from it. He leaned in to inhale her sexual perfume. 'My little pet, if you're very good, I will reward you with what you've come to crave.' He stroked the soaking wet slit between her legs. 'You know what my tongue can do for you here. Do you want it? Then you must relax and obey me now.'

"'I don't have much choice, do I, sir, what with my hands tied and all.' Again the merry twinkle in her eyes let him know she was enjoying the game as much as he.

"He loved her saucy tongue and decided he would love it even more licking his sac. Climbing on the bed and crouching above her, he lowered his testicles to her mouth. 'Taste me. Bathe me with your tongue from base to tip,' he ordered."

Again the countess paused to check on her listener. She had Christopher's rapt attention and that of his cock, too. The bulge in the front of his breeches was monumental. "Do you like the story?"

"Tied up? He has her tied to his bed? I never imagined such a thing."

"Never?" She raised an eyebrow. "Not in all your fantasies has such an idea occurred?"

His face was bright red, and she knew it wasn't heat from the fire. "It's so wrong, to treat a woman like that, to demean her by restraining and forcing her to perform lewd sexual acts."

"Ah, but in this story, it is a game the dairymaid chooses to play. With each passing chapter their sexual games grow more intense as they discover deeper levels of pleasure. But you're right. Forcing a woman to surrender and endure subjugation or humiliation is terrible— although some men seem to find it erotically pleasing. The scenario in this story is only acceptable because it's a mutual game with two players. There's the difference. Do you understand?"

He nodded. His tongue darted out to wet his lips. "A game like that. Would it be possible...? I mean, could you ever imagine yourself in such a...a position?"

Flashes of memories burst in her mind, and her hands clenched on the book. Her history with her husband had prevented her from ever wanting to indulge in bondage as sexual play, although she sometimes enjoyed reading about it. She'd had enough of real mistreatment to make her leery of ever putting herself into such a vulnerable position.

"I've played the part of the baron on occasion with some of my lovers," she finally said.

Chris's eyes widened again.

"Does that surprise you? That a man might enjoy being tied up?" She hadn't yet introduced him to the silken cords she kept in her wardrobe. There'd been enough other sex games to occupy them.

"No." He paused. "I mean, yes, it does. I know you've had many lovers and many experiences in your life that I can't even imagine, but I didn't know a woman could tie a man down and...do things to him."

She tilted her head, regarding him. "Would you like to try that tonight?"

"It sounds pleasurable, but honestly, I'd rather be the baron than the milkmaid. Could we play at that do you think?" His phrasing was so polite, he might have been asking for scones with tea.

"I don't care for being tied up," she said succinctly.

"I promise I would treat you very gently. I would never hurt you, Meredith. But I would so love to see you like that, stretched out on the bed with your wrists and ankles..." There was a soft click as he swallowed. "...tied. Could you trust me?"

Her own throat was suddenly dry, her pulse throbbing in her temples, wrists and sex. To be tied again, by choice this time and with no painful tortures or degrading words heaped upon her... Could she submit to such a thing? It

122

would be the ultimate test of the strength of will she prided herself on. Although she told herself she'd moved past the things Stephan had done to her, the truth was she was still haunted, might always be haunted by the count's cruelties. Maybe this was a way to finally put away her past.

"All right." Her stomach rolled with nausea, but perversely her pussy clenched in excitement. "You may tie me up."

Chapter Nine

Before he looped the silken cord around her wrist, he caressed her hand, wrist and forearm. His light touch stimulated her skin, sending tingles throughout her entire nude body. He kissed the pads of her fingers and palm, tickling her with his hot breath and the vibration of his murmured words. "You are so beautiful."

His tongue lapped over the pulse beating in her wrist and then up her inner arm to the crook of her elbow. Meredith shivered. "Mm. Tickles."

After kissing his way back down to her wrist, he pulled away and wrapped the cord around her sensitized flesh. He pulled it tight and knotted it, then extended her arm above her head toward the bedpost.

She craned her neck to the side so she could watch him fasten the other end of rope to the post. Her arm was stretched taut, but not uncomfortably so.

"Good?" he asked, taking a moment to sit beside her and caress her face.

"All right."

He kissed her mouth while his hand trailed down her

torso to her sex. With deft fingers he toyed with her clitoris, teasing it from its little hood to full erection. When he had her gasping into his mouth and thrusting toward his hand, Chris rose and walked around to the other side of the bed.

He gave that hand and arm the same treatment, a long slow stroke from shoulder to wrist followed by kisses and caresses. He looped the cord around her wrist and pulled it tight, stretching her arm toward the other post.

Again he paused to admire her and to check that she was feeling all right before moving down to her feet. He grasped one ankle and gave it the same loving treatment as he had her hands, wiggling her toes and trailing a fingernail along the arch of her foot.

"Stop!" she squealed, twisting and kicking her foot to get away.

"No more tickling. I promise." He kissed the bottom of her foot and her ankle, then lassoed it with a coil of gold and tied it to the far right bedpost. "Just one more. Are you ready for it?" he asked as he bent to the task of tying her last foot. He secured it to the post, leaving her legs spread wide, her pussy open and vulnerable.

He stood, arms folded, gazing at her. Meredith's skin prickled and burned all over as if she had a low-grade fever. Even though Chris had seen her naked many times, there was a vulnerability about being on display, tied hand and foot and laid open for a man who was still completely clothed. It was as if, metaphorically, she had no place to hide from his searching eyes. She felt he could see more than her body, that her inner secrets were somehow revealed.

"What are you going to do with me, sir?" she tried to adopt the saucy, flirting tone of the dairymaid in the erotic story, but her words sounded much more serious than she'd intended. A little tremble in her voice kept them from being a joke.

"I'm going to give you pleasure, Meredith. That's all. I'm going to practice the techniques you've taught me." He smiled, and her nervousness dissipated at the sweetness in his face. "And maybe discover a few new tricks of my own."

He went to her wardrobe and returned with a silk scarf. Once more he sat beside her on the bed, his weight pulling her body toward him, stretching the restraints on her right side. As he leaned to cover her eyes with the scarf and tie it around her head, she rolled her head away on the pillow. "I'm not sure about this."

"Please." His blue gaze was gentle. "You must trust me."

Reluctantly she nodded, and then she was blind as the material cut off her vision with a soft whisper of silk. He tied the scarf at the side of her head so she wouldn't be lying on a hard knot. The trailing ends of the fabric lay over her shoulder and brushed her skin lightly.

As she grew used to the darkness, her other senses heightened. She listened carefully to the sound of Chris walking across the room. What was he getting now? What might he do to her? She shifted and pulled at the cords binding her wrists, abruptly and desperately anxious to escape. He might burn or whip her, squeeze, twist or clamp her genitals and breasts, and there wasn't anything she could do to stop him.

Such things could be sexually stimulating if one was a willing participant, but Meredith had had the misfortune of suffering tortures from an unloving man. His cock had been forced, unwelcome, into all of her orifices, and she'd suffered humiliating words as well as painful treatment. Now, alone in the darkness behind her blindfold, she imagined Stephan was there in the room, ready to hurt her again.

"No!" she called. "I don't like this. I want to stop."

"Are you afraid, Meredith?" It was Chris's amiable voice, but deeper and roughened by lust. "It's just me. I promise you nothing bad will happen." His hands stroked her body up and down. His lips nibbled at her jaw and throat before settling on her mouth. He kissed her lightly, then deeper, tongue delving between her lips to find hers and urge it to play. When he pulled away, he whispered, "I'll take the blindfold and bindings off if you want me to."

"No. Not yet. I'm all right now. Just, please, keep talking to me so I know it's you."

"All right." He didn't ask who she thought he might be. She'd told him a little of her husband, so he probably knew.

He resumed touching her, thumbs tracing her collarbones, hands cupping her breasts and toying with the nipples. "You know you're safe. I only want to make you feel good." He talked on in a reassuring litany, while his hands massaged the tension from her shoulders and arms. By the time he'd kneaded all the way down her torso and each leg, then back up to her crotch, she was relaxed and aroused. Her sex felt like a lump of butter melting from solid into warm, slippery liquid.

She moaned and shifted, pulling at her legs and arms, testing the restraints. When she tugged against them, they held, but it no longer made her feel like thrashing in a panic to get away. She was comfortable and content to give control to Chris, who continued murmuring endearments and compliments about her beauty, cleverness and strength of will, all the while touching her in delightful ways.

Meredith felt him kneel between her legs, his hands resting on the insides of her thighs. She raised her pelvis toward what she knew was coming. When his mouth touched her sex, her senses were so attuned that it sent a powerful jolt through her. The lips of her aching pussy were swollen, and without the distraction of sight, his kiss on her flushed labia was like the striking of a tuning fork—vibrations arching through her in waves.

She moaned softly and raised her hips even farther off the bed, straining her arms and legs to push higher, yearning for his tongue on her clit. But Chris wasn't going to make it so easy. He teased her, kissing her inner thighs, licking the crease where thigh met torso, nibbling with careful teeth at her folds, then dipping his tongue deep inside her. He lapped her juices, spread them from her quim to her clit and swirled around it—but just once.

Meredith moaned louder, encouraging him to give her more, but he left her nib erect and aching for touch. He rose from the bed and crossed the room. She whined in disappointment and listened to the soft sounds he made somewhere over by the dresser. Her curiosity about his actions now held anticipation rather than fear.

His footsteps trod back toward the bed across the heavy carpet, one of the floorboards creaking under his weight. Now he stood beside the bed again, and Meredith drew in a breath, waiting...waiting.

Something soft and fragrant brushed her face. It tickled over her forehead, cheek and lips. A feather? She inhaled and identified the object by fragrance. A rose! He had taken one of the roses from the bouquet on the dresser and was stroking her throat, her chest, each thrusting breast and her twitching belly. The pink roses had been cut several days ago and were completely open and beginning to shed petals. The rich, sweet smell of the flower suffused her senses and every cell of her flesh felt alive and sensitized to the petals' touch. Having her vision removed enhanced these sensations. When Chris swept the soft petals all the way from her instep to her inner thigh, her leg shook, and when he stroked it over her yawning pussy, tickling it around the stiffened lips, her whole body convulsed.

"Ohhhh! Please," she begged.

Still he wasn't finished with his game. He brought the rose back up to her face. Her own scent was now mingled with the heady floral aroma. The flower teased back and forth across her lips until they opened as though for a lover's kiss. A moment later, Chris's mouth fastened on hers once more. He kissed her breathless before pulling away. "You can't imagine how beautiful you look like this."

Meredith felt something featherlight land on her chest, her breasts and belly, and settle gently on her pulsing sex. The sweet scent of roses grew even stronger, filling her until she felt she was part of the essence of the rose itself. He had showered her with petals, sprinkled them over her body. Imagining how she must look to him, spread open like a full bloom herself, she felt as beautiful as he'd told her she was—and in much more than a superficial sense. Meredith was well aware she was an attractive woman, but the beauty she felt now was deeper than appearance. With his soft caresses and baptism of petals, Chris made her feel a deep sense of her inner beauty and worth, which, despite her bold talk and confident manner, had been lacking in her for a very long time.

"You are a goddess," he whispered.

She felt his weight lift from the bed beside her, heard his footsteps and a rustle of clothing. At last he was undressing. Her slightly numb fingers gripped the cords holding her arms over her head. Her toes flexed and her ankles pulled against the bindings on them. She eagerly awaited his body settling between her legs. Surely he wouldn't keep her in suspense any longer. Her pussy clenched and released in steady beats, yawning wide and begging for fulfillment.

He climbed onto the foot of the bed. Once more his

hands stroked her legs from ankle to thighs. His thumbs traced her labia, and his mouth lowered to kiss her there again.

"Are you ready for me, Meredith?" he teased after he'd licked her until she was writhing against her restraints and moaning loudly.

"Yesss," she hissed. "Please...fuck me." The harsh gutter term always made Chris even more eager. She knew this about him, having seen his increased response when she used it, the shocked widening of his eyes and intake of breath. She might be tied down, but it didn't mean all the power was in his hands. Meredith knew how to rouse his lust with just her words.

"I want you inside me right now. I need to feel you filling me with your big, thick cock. Fuck me, sir. Fuck me deep and hard." She smiled smugly as she listened to the telltale quickening of his breath.

There was a long pause before he murmured in a strangled voice, "Not yet. I'll see to your pleasure first, my sweet prisoner." And then his tongue was back at her clit, relentlessly stroking the quivering nubbin of flesh until waves of shimmering pleasure burst through her.

Meredith cried out and arched her back, lifting impossibly high as though she would fly off the bed and only the four bonds held her down. Her muscles ached with the torturous acrobatics, but she barely felt them since her entire being was suffused with sparkling shards of bliss raining down like the rose petals. Such intense delight and emotion from the simple touch of his tongue.

What shaped men and made them so very different that one would revel in giving her satisfaction and joy while another withheld even the barest scrap of pleasure from her and delighted in causing pain?

When her body had stopped bucking and came to rest at last on the rumpled sheets, Chris kissed her inner thighs and crawled over her, covering her body with his. His erection nudged at her dripping quim, but he paused before pushing inside.

"Do your arms and legs hurt? Do you want me to loosen them now?" His breath touched her cheek, and she smelled herself on the whiff of air.

"No. I'm fine," she assured him. She wanted to add how very grateful she was that he'd bothered to ask, but kept the thought in her heart instead.

"All right, then." The weight of his torso on hers forced her body deeper into the mattress and added strain to her limbs, but she didn't mind the bit of pain along with her pleasure. The discomfort was erotically fulfilling and she welcomed it. He kept most of his weight off her, braced on his arms. They dug into the pillow on either side of her head. He brushed his lips across her perspiring forehead and then, in a sudden thrust, he entered her body.

Her channel was slick and ready for him. Her inner muscles clenched around his cock, pulling him inside. He thrust balls deep into her with a satisfied grunt.

"You feel so good in me," she murmured, encouraging him with her voice since she couldn't clutch his ass and pull him into her as she normally would. "Your cock is so wide. It fills me completely."

Every man loved to hear his cock praised, and Chris was no exception. Her continued murmuring about his length and girth and her explicit description of his cock's appearance when she held it in her hands were enough to whip him to a frenzy. Very quickly Chris's careful, measured strokes became erratic. He thrust faster, and as hard and deep as she commanded.

The wonderful sensation of being filled coupled with the sensual sounds of his desperate groans. Oh how she loved the reverberation of masculine need growled low in his throat. It made her skin prickle and her pussy clench even harder. Deep inside he struck a chord, like one note on a piano played over and over again. Meredith felt a new wave of pleasure gathering in her, but before it could crash against the shore of her consciousness, Chris thrust once more, then froze, shuddering. She wanted to throw her arms around his back and hold him while he came, but could only lie there helpless as he trembled against her.

One last nudge of his cock and her body abruptly peaked, too. The single note turned into a symphony with blaring brass, sensuous strings and seductive woodwinds. A full-blown orchestra erupted within her and she thrashed and wailed along with the music. When the last note had died away, she exhaled a long, unsteady breath.

Chris's full weight now pinned her to the bed and the pressure on her arms and legs had become excruciating. She shifted beneath him.

He lifted his head from her shoulder, raised his body off hers and peeled the blindfold back from her eyes. "All right?"

She nodded.

Rising from the bed, he untied her wrists and ankles, then rubbed them briskly, bringing the blood coursing back into her hands and feet. The prickling reminded her of when she used to come in from playing in the snow as a child and her skin had burned from the warmth indoors. Her long-ago husband had never bothered to aid her when he'd finally released her. Usually he'd tossed her weakened body from his bed, sending her staggering back to her own room on leaden legs, finished with her—until the next time.

"What's the matter?" Chris stood at the foot of the bed, rubbing her ankles and the arches and heels of her feet. A frown creased his forehead as he put her foot down and climbed onto the bed to lie beside her. "You didn't like it?"

She smiled. "No. It was good. Very powerful. But it brought back some memories I'd done my best to dispel." She turned and nestled back against his body, pulling his arm around her.

He hugged her and kissed the back of her shoulder. "I'm sorry. I didn't mean to make you unhappy."

Meredith reached over her shoulder to touch his cheek. "I'm not, really. Maybe these were memories I needed to acknowledge in order to get rid of them forever." She realized her words were true. She felt unfettered and free in a way she never had before. All of her years of pursuing financial success and sexual pleasure hadn't brought the peace that filled her at this moment. What was this warm glow in her center that seemed to spread to every part of her being?

"I love you," Chris murmured as he smoothed a hand over her shoulder.

Meredith's heart plummeted. *That* was the warm glow she felt. That word she swore she didn't believe in had seized hold of her and held her fast. Love? Impossible! This wasn't what she'd agreed to. It was supposed to be a simple exchange of favors; she'd deflower the virginal Whitby and teach him to be more socially adept and in return Lord Whitby would ensure the bill she needed was passed. It was bad enough that Chris was developing feelings for her she'd have to crush. Now, it appeared, she had some very strong emotions for him, and that would never do.

"Excuse me." She slid from under his protective arm and out of bed.

He grasped her hand before she could escape. "Is everything all right?"

Forcing a smile, she turned toward him. "I simply need a few moments alone to refresh myself." His frown smoothed after she blew him a kiss from her fingertips.

She removed the chamber pot from beneath the bed and retreated into the privacy of her dressing room. With the door safely closed behind her, she leaned against the wall, her head in her hands. The elated afterglow of sex evaporated, leaving her anxious and upset.

She assured herself that the warm, safe feeling of completion she'd experienced just now was *not* love, but merely residual passion from an exceptionally intense bout of lovemaking. Sometimes the body was tricky like that. Her brain had misread the feeling. That was all. Because love, as she well knew, did not exist, and it was a dreadful mistake to place one's hope, faith, and trust in a man—even a man as seemingly kind and thoughtful as Christopher Whitby.

No. The amorous game she was playing had suddenly gotten far too complicated. It was time to end this affair, to return to London and release her little fish back into the stream. With his new sexual confidence and the air of authority he now wore like a mantle, Chris would be sure to attract the right fisherwoman, who'd land him and his title for her daughter. That was as it should be. There was no future for him with Meredith. A long-term affair wasn't possible, and a marriage? Out of the question. Not only had she forsworn to ever again enter that estate, but a widow with a tarnished reputation was not an appropriate match for a young man of good family. It would be far better for Christopher to settle down with a proper young lady, who could run his household and bear him children while he pursued his botanical studies.

Her heart clenched at the familial picture she'd painted. What kind of father would Chris be? Perhaps a little distracted by academia, but patient, loving and eager to teach his children. Meredith hated the woman in her vision for having what she could not.

She imagined her own future: shallow dalliances and coolly planned business deals. Neither prospect amused or interested her any longer.

"Meredith? Are you coming back?" Chris's voice floated from the other room, half teasing and half concerned.

"I'll be right there." She quickly relieved herself and washed up. She paused to face her reflection in the mirror before returning to the bedroom. Her hair tumbled wildly around her face and her eyes were huge and dark.

"You will not be selfish and use this man any longer," she said. "You will do what's right and set him free just as he has done for you tonight."

Pushing her hair back, she turned and strode into the bedroom. She paused in the dressing room doorway and smiled at the man lying in her bed. "Darling, let's talk about London. I think it's really past time we returned home, don't you?"

Chapter Ten

Chris held the pot of *Oenothera* in the crook of one arm, sheltering the pink blossoms from the jostling crowd. He should've taken a cab after leaving Aunt Alberta's house.

His mother had been aghast when he'd handed her into the carriage, then explained he had an errand to run and would see her at home later. "But you didn't mention anything before. What's so important that you can't accompany me home first?"

"Goodbye, Mother." It had felt good to close the door on her never-ending complaints. He'd accompanied her on a social call to his great-aunt as requested, but now he was finished with family obligations and had more important things to do.

Although he'd only been home for a few days, he already missed Meredith unbearably. He'd missed her from the moment they'd kissed goodbye and he'd climbed into the carriage heading back to the city, much against his will.

He'd tried to get her to postpone their return, citing the fact that their greenhouse project was only partially finished, but she'd resisted his pleas. The day after that amazing night when she'd allowed him to tie her up, Meredith had practically thrown him out of her house. She'd had her servants pack his bags and load them on the waiting carriage.

"I'm sorry, my dear, but I've lingered in the country too long. I have business affairs to see to in London." Her voice was breezy and her smile distant. "I can't play house with you any longer. It's time we both returned to our real lives."

Her words had cut like knife blades, but Chris knew she didn't really mean them. The brittle façade she presented to the world wasn't the real Meredith. He knew her better than that now.

And he knew she loved him, whether she would admit to it or not.

She must. No one could put on such an act. He'd felt her love in every caress and kiss. He'd seen it shining in her eyes and in the small smile that trembled at the corners of her mouth. Women having casual affairs didn't behave the way she had with him. Did they?

৪০

Meredith's London home was only a few streets away from his parents' house. Knowing she was there made it nearly impossible to keep away. But he'd taken what she'd said to heart and given her a week to see her friends and catch up on her business affairs. He didn't want to be smothering, especially when he felt his hold on her was so fragile. He couldn't force her to want him as much as he wanted her, but he believed if he was careful and patient with her he could get her to trust him. She was rather like a wild bird that must be cajoled into alighting on an outstretched hand.

However, today he'd decided he couldn't stay apart from her any longer. Memories of her soft, raven hair, her misty gray eyes and delicate, pale skin sliding over his own had him in a state of perpetual arousal. He missed her voice, her laugh, her caustic remarks. And, oh God, how he missed her mouth, the petal smooth lips and warm wetness as she kissed him or engulfed his shaft. Damn it! He held the potted plant lower to hide the burgeoning erection filling the front of his breeches.

A gust of wind blew down the street, swirling dust, soot and trash in a small whirlwind that buffeted the passers-by. Chris turned his body to shield the delicate plant from the cold breeze. He really should've taken a cab after stopping at the florist shop, for the plant's sake if not his own, but he'd felt so buoyant and energized he'd wanted to walk the five blocks to Meredith's home on St. Augustine.

The crowd of people thinned as he turned a corner and entered a residential neighborhood of tall white homes protected by ornate wrought-iron fences. The streets were as impeccable as the homes. No grit or trash here where street sweepers were employed to keep the wealthy from being subjected to the city's filth.

At last Chris found the address for which he'd been searching. Her house looked like every other in the row of imposing buildings. There was none of the character of her country estate, and for a moment he froze with his hand on the doorbell, wondering if he'd made a mistake. The woman he'd come to know and love in the country might be a different person from the woman who lived in this stately home. It seemed impossible that she'd be the same. Maybe he should have sent a note first to announce his visit.

Another errant breeze blew past, nearly lifting his hat from his head. He glanced at the flowering plant in his arms, chosen for the color, which so reminded him of Meredith. The blossoms were the same rosy-peach as her delectable labia and with a similar plumpness. He thought she would see the symbolism and be amused by it.

Chris smiled. Of course she would welcome him! She hadn't completely ended their relationship when they parted, merely told him she wanted time alone to think and he should do the same. Well, he had thought. A lot. Always of her. And he knew she was exactly what he wanted—who he wanted to spend the rest of his life with in whatever capacity that might be, as a wife or a lover.

He was prepared to tell her that today, to proclaim his love again but explain that he wouldn't demand she marry him since her individuality was so important to her. Of course, it would be wonderful if she trusted him with the gift of herself, as she'd done the night she'd allowed him to tie her to the bed. But if she could only accept him as a long-term lover, he'd be content with that.

Twisting the doorbell, he listened to the ring sound inside the house. A few moments later, a black-coated butler with a stiff white collar opened the front door. "Good afternoon, sir."

"Hello. I'm here to see la Comtesse de Chevalier."

"Madame is with another guest at the moment." The man's face was impassive.

"I'll wait. She'll want to see me. Tell her Christopher Whitby has come to call."

There was a flicker of expression across the butler's face before he stepped back to let him inside. "Very well, sir. If you would wait in the parlor, I'll announce you to madame when there is an opportunity."

The plant in his arms was unwieldy. Chris wished he'd purchased something smaller and more standard like a bouquet, but he'd imagined this evening primrose planted near the bench in the conservatory where it would fill the shaded area under the trees. It had looked so perfect there in his imagination that he just had to have it. He hoped Meredith would love it, too.

The butler took his hat and topcoat and showed him to the parlor, which was as stiff and formal as that in any other London town house. It didn't seem to reflect Meredith at all. Chris set the plant on the floor and sat on the edge of the hard, horsehair sofa to wait. He glanced around at the numerous paintings on the damask-covered walls, the gilt trim around the ornate mirror over the fireplace mantel, the objects d'art lining the mantel, the little tables also scattered with trinkets and the furniture built for decoration more than comfort. This room was definitely not the product of "his" informal and relaxed Meredith. Perhaps this was the mask she put on for society, keeping her true nature hidden.

Chris rose to wander the room. As he stood before one of the tall windows, he caught a glimpse of a corner of the garden at the back of the house, and in the garden, the flash of a blue skirt. His heart rose at the sight of his beloved. He wouldn't wait for the butler to announce him, but surprise her in the garden. He imagined coming up behind her and wrapping his arms around her. She would shriek in surprise, then whirl to face him, throwing her arms around his neck and kissing him.

The image of her reaction warmed him through. He ached to hold her in his arms again and quickly found his way down the hall and out a side door leading to the garden.

The air was fresh after the stifling enclosure of the house, and the heat of the sun beat heavily on his head. Chris wondered if the servants in Meredith's city home were as close-lipped as the estate staff. If he and the countess were inclined to enjoy some pastoral coupling in the garden right now, would there be eyes peering from behind drawn drapes? The idea actually made his cock grow stiffer. He smiled at his fancy, and stepped away from the shadow of the house to walk beneath the foliage of a young elm.

The musical sound of Meredith's voice coming from behind an evergreen bush made his smile widen, but he

143

froze when a male voice responded. His first thought was that he should have expected some of her London friends would be male. Following that came the instant realization that it was his father's voice. Shock rooted him to the spot. Why would Father be in Meredith's garden?

Perhaps the old man had come to warn the countess away from his son. Lord Whitby would not approve of the ill-reputed woman as a daughter-in-law, no matter how titled and wealthy she was, especially since she couldn't bear heirs, which seemed to be his prime desire in life. Before Chris could conjecture further, his father spoke.

"Overall, I'm mightily pleased with the changes you've wrought in the lad and in such a short time. I see a bolder, more confident side of him than I'd imagined he possessed."

"Christopher is the same man he always was. He only needed a boost of confidence to bring forth his true nature."

"Well, we'll see how it translates at the ball tomorrow night. I hope you've broken him out of his shyness enough that he'll finally pursue a young lady or two. The lad might produce an heir in my lifetime after all!"

Meredith moved, and Chris saw bits of blue through the leaves that shielded the pair from his view. "Sir, I can't guarantee what he might do. You asked me to draw him out of his reserve and I believe that's been accomplished. But I can't make him any more willing to attend balls or to court whomever you select for him. That desire must come from within him."

"And perhaps the lad has visions of someone a little older and more experienced blinding him right now, eh? Perhaps you've done your work a little too well. If I don't get the results I expected, then you can't expect to receive my help on that bill. I'll neither support it nor use my influence in your favor."

Chris was numb, his brain trying to interpret the words. They sounded exactly like a business transaction. His heart shriveled like a dying leaf in the long pause before the countess spoke again.

"I understand," she replied coolly. "I tried to make sure your son understood our arrangement was merely a temporary liaison, but perhaps I needed to make it even more clear. I'll be attending the ball tomorrow night and I'll illustrate the lesson so there can be no mistake. Will that do?"

"I don't know." Father's tone was arrogant. "It all depends on the results, doesn't it? If I see the behavior I want in my son, I'll ensure the millworkers' bill goes through."

"Very well." Her quiet reply was like a slippered foot stepping down and crushing the dried leaf of his heart into powder for the wind to blow away.

A flash of black to the left and a soft clearing of a throat caught Chris's attention. The butler interrupted the conversation. "Excuse me, madame. You have another guest, who insisted on waiting for you in the parlor."

Chris's throat constricted, and a jolt of energy set his legs moving away from the scene of his humiliation, back toward the house. He could not face her, not now. Behind him, he heard the countess say, "If you'll excuse me, sir, I believe this discussion is concluded."

His father replied, "I will speak to you again when our agreement is complete."

Slipping in the side door, Chris walked quickly down the hall toward the foyer, located his hat on a side table, his coat on a tree, and put them on. His hands trembled as he fumbled with the doorknob. He finally got it open and burst out onto the front stoop. The door closed behind him as he took the steps two at a time and nearly raced down the street.

Hailing the first hansom cab he saw, he climbed inside.

The driver looked over his shoulder. "Where to, sir?"

He had no answer. He was unable to bear the idea of going home where his father had betrayed him—his privacy, his honor, his trust. Chris had never imagined the depths to which his father would sink to accomplish his goal of securing an heir. And Meredith—no, the countess. He could no longer think of her as Meredith, who had been an illusion put on for his benefit. She had been the one thing that ever truly felt like home. So where could he go now?

"To the Botanical Gardens, please."

&)

Walking the white gravel paths of the Gardens had always been rather like a meditation for Chris. He would breathe deeply of the pungent earth and green plants that enriched the air and stroll the familiar walk while mentally reciting a relaxing litany of the plants he passed. He didn't need to read the little placards labeling them to know their names. They were more familiar to him than the names of the people whose world he inhabited.

Lady Darlington-Smythe, Lord Joseph Abernathy, the third Earl of Stokes, James Tavington and his wife, Lady Marian—those were his mother's litany, the important details that gave meaning to her life. His father's would be a list of club names: White's, Brooks' and Boodle's as well as more unsavory gambling hells like Crockford's and The Black Ram.

Everyone had something that gave meaning to his or her life, no matter how shallow or pointless it might seem to others. But today Chris trudged listlessly past *Acer triflorum*, *Morus alba* and *Prunus serotina* without even looking at them. They meant nothing to him now. His chest felt like a gaping wound and his soul as arid as a desert.

He had a new litany now, but it didn't soothe him. It was a list of Meredith: the way her left eyebrow was a fraction higher than her right, the cluster of freckles shaped like Orion on her thigh, her mingled shrieks and laughter when he tackled her to the bed and showered her with kisses, the low murmur of her voice when she confided in him, her smile when he presented her with a wildflower, the light in her eyes when she beheld their joint handiwork in her newly refurbished greenhouse.

Everything he knew about Meredith was in question now. How much of her had been real and how much a sham? As they'd grown closer, he'd convinced himself she truly loved him, but then she'd warned him all along their affair was temporary. He should have listened for it was the one sure truth in the midst of her lies.

When he looked back, her insistence on teaching him to dance and play cards, her hints about exuding confidence to win a woman's attention all made more sense. She was tutoring him as his father had requested, attempting to turn him into a standard man of his class. She hadn't even been very circumspect about the fact she was grooming him for society, so he shouldn't be so surprised.

Chris took a seat in the Japanese garden. He gazed at the peahens that roamed free, pecking for seeds on the ground, while the peacock fanned his tail feathers in an attempt to earn their attention.

Meredith had done her job well. He did possess skills now he hadn't before, and not only in bed. He knew how to flirt and wouldn't become tongue-tied if he had to chat with a woman. He could dance and look at her as if she was the most important thing in the world. With Meredith, those things had been easy, but he was sure he could manufacture the same effect with any girl.

An idea began to take shape. His hurt and despair mingled with anger, adding up to an overwhelming desire for revenge. He would be exactly the kind of man his father and the countess had wanted him to be—for one night, at least.

He would go to the Overtons' ball, which his mother had been harassing him to attend ever since his return to London. Meredith would be there. She would want to see the results of her tutelage, so he would give her a show.

He'd wear a new suit of clothes and take society by storm, dancing with every eligible young lady in the room and charming them all. And when he passed Meredith in the midst of the crowd, he would glance at her and then pass her by.

Chapter Eleven

"It's for the best. It really is for the best." Saying it aloud didn't make Meredith feel the truth of it anymore than had repeating the same mantra silently for the past twenty-four hours. She stared at her reflection in the mirror, the pale bosom rising from the lace of her décolletage, the black velvet choker with the red garnet emphasizing her slender throat, hair piled high and pinned with a garnet-studded comb.

Her lips were rouged red, the bright color a stark contrast to her white skin. Her mouth was drawn tight and slightly down-turned at the corners. She forced herself to relax and manufacture a smile. When she saw Christopher tonight, she would have to play the part she'd set for herself and not let him see the melancholy that clenched her heart and turned it to a cold, hard stone.

But she couldn't suppress the sadness in her eyes. She blinked her dark lashes to whisk away the mist of tears. "It's what he needed to hear. There was no future for us."

Meredith had no doubt Chris had overheard her speaking to his father in the garden yesterday. After she'd seen the elder Whitby out the door, she'd turned to Hawkins and asked who was waiting for her in the parlor. It wasn't like the butler not to tell her a visitor's name.

"The Honorable Mr. Whitby, madame. I didn't think it wise to announce his presence in front of his father."

She'd missed him terribly the past few days and had often considered sending a note to him, but knew pushing him away was for his own good. Her heart had begun doing acrobatics in her chest, flipping, twisting, then rising in a combination of nervous anxiety and eagerness at the prospect of seeing him. It wasn't until she entered the parlor and saw the pink-blossomed plant but no Christopher that fear joined her mix of emotions.

"You left him here?"

"Yes, madame. I waited only a few minutes to interrupt your conversation with Lord Whitby, but perhaps the younger Whitby grew impatient and left."

"No." The word was barely a murmur, all she could push out past the thickness in her throat. In that instant she was absolutely certain that Chris had found his own way to the garden and overheard at least part of her conference with his father. Her hand rose to cover her mouth and her stomach lurched. "No."

She imagined the scene as clearly as if witnessing it from above: the young man standing out of sight behind some trees, listening to a discussion he was never meant to hear. What exactly had they said—that his father had practically hired her like a whore to seduce him? What in the world had made her agree to such an arrangement?

For a woman who prided herself on following her own desires and dictates, she'd allowed Whitby too much power over her. She'd taken on the project of Chris because she was intrigued by the challenge, but also because Whitby's influence on the millworkers' bill would benefit her financially. It had appeared a practical arrangement with entertaining side benefits when she accepted the offer. Now it seemed dirty, underhanded and utterly cruel.

"Oh dear," she sighed, rubbing her hand across her forehead. The woman in the mirror did the same. "You're despicable. You deserve to have him hate you."

She finished preparing for the ball, all the while vacillating between the idea of attending or staying home and hiding in her bed for about a month. After what he'd heard yesterday, Christopher probably wouldn't attend the event. He surely wouldn't want to see her there. But if he was there... Oh, how she dreaded seeing the hurt and betrayal in his eyes before he shunned her by turning away.

Or it would be worse. He might confront her, try to convince her that the time they'd spent together had meant something. He might profess his love again. She couldn't bear hearing that. Better to crawl under her covers and hide.

But a half hour later, the countess was handed into her carriage by her footman, and ten minutes after that she disembarked at the Overtons' house. She removed her wrap in the foyer, where it was whisked away by the attending servant, and entered the rose-decked, crystal and gold ballroom. Mirrors on one wall served to make the already massive room and substantial crowd appear even larger. Music filled the air, and a steady murmur of voices rose above it. A few couples were already dancing. The charge of energy and excitement in the air, usually pleasurable to her, only enhanced Meredith's nervous nausea tonight as she scanned the guests, searching for Chris.

Perspiration broke out, not only on her palms, but all over her flesh from anxiety coupled with the heat generated by many bodies. She longed and dreaded to see him with the powerful strength of a girlish crush. It was terrible how out of control her emotions were. Memories of their erotic play had her pussy clenching wetly, her breasts tender and aching, while recollections of his low voice, his kind smile and gentle hands made her heart palpitate. Fear that he hadn't come to the ball mingled with fear that he had.

Then, across the room, she caught a glimpse of a sandy blond head and his profile as he turned.

Meredith froze and her breath caught. Oh God, this was a mistake! She should've met and talked with him before tonight. A confrontation in this venue was going to be a disaster. She swallowed and clenched her hands by her sides at the same moment that Christopher's gaze fell on her, paused...and swept past as if he didn't recognize her.

Perhaps he simply hadn't seen her. Meredith took a step in his direction.

"My dear Countess! Where have you been? It's been so dreary in town without you." A hand fell on her wrist, and she turned to face Rupert Chadwick, an old friend and occasional lover. His thin moustache lifted as he smiled, and his royal blue coat made his eyes sparkle even more brilliantly.

"Rupert, how are you?" She clasped his hands and air-kissed each cheek, catching another glimpse of Chris over the man's shoulder. He was escorting the Overtons' eldest daughter, Elspeth, onto the dance floor. Jealousy stabbed her as he slipped a hand around the young woman's waist, pulling her into his embrace. They gracefully moved into the stream of dancers circling the floor.

"...but then, she never was much of a fashion plate. Don't you think?" As Meredith stepped back, Rupert turned to see who she was looking at over his shoulder.

"See someone you know—or want to know better?" He laughed. He knew her sexual proclivities well and had attended to them in the past. Perhaps he was hoping for a quick téte-a-téte in a side room tonight, but that wasn't going to happen. Meredith had never felt less sexual desire.

No. That wasn't true. Her body was reacting strongly, but not to the man standing beside her. "I believe it's time for a dance." She grasped his hand and tugged him toward the floor. She needed to get closer to Chris, to see if he was actually ignoring her or merely hadn't seen her. *And what then?* A quiet inner voice tried to inject reason into the wild jumble of emotions coursing through her.

154

Your mission is to cut him. Do you simply want to make sure that you're the one to do it first? Are you that proud and petty?

Rupert didn't ask any more questions, simply swung her onto the dance floor, and soon they were in the thick of the glittering crowd of dancers. Meredith caught a flash of Chris and his partner whirling by. He was talking and the girl was laughing, her face tilted toward his and her eyes shining. And why not? He cut a dashing figure tonight. He was impeccably dressed and groomed and carried himself with a bold assurance. His demeanor was the polar opposite of the distracted, uncertain air he'd presented when Meredith first met him. Was this even "her" Christopher? He seemed so different.

Once again, their eyes briefly met. His penetrating stare pierced her before he looked away. Her chest felt as if he'd stuck a knife into it. There was no doubt he'd seen her this time, but his expression was cold and remote, as if she was someone he'd been introduced to once a long time ago instead of the woman who'd recently taught him what passion meant. How dare he brush her off? Even as she knew her burst of anger was irrational, for surely she'd earned his disgust, Meredith couldn't control the sudden fury that filled her.

Her partner leaned close. "Who's the young buck? Do you want me to help make him jealous?" Rupert nuzzled her neck a moment before pulling away without ever missing a step in the dance.

Meredith gave him a brittle smile. "He's no one, just a lad I...tutored for a while, a short-lived liaison. I had to end it when his affection grew too deep." It was an effort to keep her tone light. She felt abruptly exhausted and more ready than ever to retreat from the playing field of the ballroom and curl up in the sanctuary of her bed. But she knew that even there she couldn't escape Chris. Memories of what they'd done in bed together would continue to haunt her. No man had ever gotten past her defenses and touched her so deeply before.

The dance ended, and she watched him lead his partner from the floor, the pair of them still laughing and talking. For the first time, Meredith realized it might not be Chris who was at risk of a broken heart. It was hers that was shattering into pieces at the thought of a future without him in it.

Now that she'd ruined her chances with him, now that he knew her for what she truly was and despised her, she finally acknowledged the hopeless passion she harbored for him. She would give anything to accept the love he'd so freely offered—now that there was no chance of him offering it ever again.

Meredith subjected herself to the torture of being near him, but ignored for a little while longer. No matter whom she spoke with, he was always on the periphery of her vision. She couldn't stop watching him laugh, flirt and dance with every eligible young lady in the room. His father would be so pleased, she thought dryly. Chris looked completely natural and at ease. His new assuredness attracted the women like bees to pollen. They fluttered and fussed around him while Meredith fumed. Her stomach was a cold, hard knot and she felt her facial muscles stiffen in a parody of a smile as she greeted people she knew.

Finally she couldn't take the tension any longer. She must at least speak to Chris before she left. She had to hear his voice, which she'd missed so much in the days since they'd left the country. God, why had she ever wanted to end those blissful days? She couldn't remember any longer. Why had she driven away the best man to ever stumble into her life? Fool!

She excused herself from Rupert and casually made her way through the crowd until she was near Chris and his group of admirers. Then she casually stepped backward and bumped into him, turning and steadying herself on his arm. "Excuse me... Why, Mister Whitby! What a pleasant surprise."

He stared into her face with cool blue eyes, his mouth set in a thin line. "Madame la Comtesse." He gave her a curt nod, then turned away, back toward Hortense Simon, who'd been giving a harrowing description of a near-accident on a recent carriage ride.

The tailored back of his coat seemed as big as a wall when he turned it toward Meredith, closing her off. She was aware of the young ladies' widened eyes and exchanged glances at the obvious affront. As soon as she walked away, there would be whispers at her expense and gossip circulating the room about how young Christopher Whitby had cut the Countess de Chevalier.

For one brief moment, her pride stripped and her heart open and bleeding, Meredith considered taking his arm and begging an audience, asking him to please take a turn with her in the garden. She wanted desperately to get him alone and explain herself, to suffer his rage if that's what it took to get him to talk to her, anything besides accept this dismissive silence.

But she knew she'd earned it. He was reacting from wounded pride and a damaged heart as was to be expected, and wasn't this the result she'd been moving toward all along—a complete severance of relations?

Meredith turned and slipped between two large matrons with broad bosoms and towering hair. She hid behind the bulwark of their hefty bodies, out of Chris's sight, if he should happen to glance toward her.

Locating Rupert, she made her way across the room and joined him again. "Take me someplace," she ordered, taking his arm. "This party bores me. I need some real entertainment."

"Gladly," he answered, leading her toward the door. "Anywhere you desire, madame. Your pleasure is my pleasure."

℘

The crowd at Crockford's pressed shoulder to shoulder around the gaming tables. Cigar smoke hung in a choking pall over the men in their black suits and the women in glittering diamonds and a rainbow display of satin and silk. The scent of men's hair pomades and ladies' perfumes mingled with the rancid stench of sweat. It was even worse than the crush of bodies in the ballroom.

Meredith recognized many familiar faces, slack from drink or opium, swollen with excess, jaded from indulging in every pleasure and depravity they could discover or invent. These were her friends, the people she'd come back to London to see?

The moment she and Rupert entered the main salon, she wished she'd asked him to take her someplace quiet for a drink—or ten.

"Feeling lucky tonight?" His moustache tickled her ear and his breath puffed hot against her neck. "I've had a bad run lately myself. Maybe you'd better place my bets for me." His hand pressed against her back as he propelled her toward one of the faro tables.

After betting and losing several hundred pounds on the cards in less than fifteen minutes, they moved on to hazard. The excitement and jocularity of the players gathered around the table as they bantered with wry cynicism and lost their inheritances was like the chattering of monkeys. Meredith couldn't believe she once got a thrill from the simple act of throwing dice. The foolishness of gambling no longer appealed, and her headache was growing worse.

"You were supposed to be my good luck charm, madame," Rupert teased after she'd thrown a straight succession of twos and threes, losing another few hundred pounds. Money that would've kept a working class family afloat for months.

Meredith felt a little ill as her friend pressed a glass of whiskey into her hand.

"No matter. Come on. Let's see what's going on in the fight room."

She tossed back her drink, the alcohol burning down her throat and setting a fire in her belly. She took Rupert's arm and he led her deeper into the maze of gaming rooms. Beyond the main salon were antechambers where private card games went on for hours, or even days, and fortunes were won and lost on a single hand.

But Rupert was taking her to the lower level where cockfights, dogfights and other match-ups took place. The contact of bloody combat was a visceral thrill for gentlemen whose home lives were as tidy and clean as starched linen.

Very few women were in the basement chamber of Crockford's gambling hell. Even the whores and mistresses who enjoyed gambling with their lovers were generally barred from the violence that went on below.

But the countess was an exception. She'd always gone where she wanted and done what she wanted, gaining entry even into this sacrosanct men's world.

Her stomach lurched as she saw the entertainment for the evening was a bare-knuckle fistfight between what looked like two bums someone had pulled in from the alley. They were scrawny, sickly drunks, not the brawny lads one would expect in a proper boxing match. But that was the kind of sick twist the young bucks of the ton thought was hilarious, to make japes of the poverty-stricken dregs of society.

"Oh my, who thought up this depressing tomfoolery?" Rupert chuckled and shook his head. "Quick, which one shall we back? Neither of them looks like they have much fight left in them."

The older of the two skinny men took a poke at the other and hit his chin. His opponent staggered backward into the cheering circle of men. Someone pushed him back into the fight. He earned another jab to the face that snapped his head sideways and sent blood spraying from his nose.

Meredith's stomach twisted again, and she clutched Rupert's arm. "Let's go."

"Just a moment. I want to see—"

"Now! I'm going to be ill," she whispered urgently. "Unless you want vomit on your shiny shoes."

He stared into her face. "You are quite pale. Come along then."

Rupert took her arm and led her from the room, back upstairs, through the overpowering stench and noise and finally into the blessed coolness of the night air. It was hardly fresh, this being London. The smell of coal smoke, urine and decaying garbage in the gutter, and horse dung in the street mingled in the aroma of a city.

Meredith longed for the fresh green scent of earth and plants. Why had leaving her country home ever seemed like a good idea? How had she imagined that breaking

Chris's heart was the right thing to do?

"What's the matter, darling? You don't seem yourself tonight?" Rupert stroked her hand, which was still looped through his arm and clutching his sleeve. "I know we haven't seen each other in a long time, but you appear quite changed."

"Me? Nonsense." Her laugh sounded crisp and brittle to her ears. "It was something I ate at the Overtons' atrocious buffet coupled with too little fresh air. A turn around the park in your landau and I'll be fine."

"Absolutely. Then back to your place?" Rupert's eyebrow raised and Meredith had no doubt what he was asking about.

"We shall see." She lowered her eyelids and gave him a coquettish smile, despising herself even as she flirted. Why was she doing it? She didn't want this man. Not even for one night. She wanted nothing more than to go home, fall into bed and sleep for a thousand years.

But a doggedly determined part of her insisted on living up to her outrageous reputation. She would be the cold-hearted woman Christopher thought she was, proving him right, but also proving to herself that she didn't care.

The open-carriage ride through the park actually did make her feel better. The stars glowed overhead except where the dark foliage of trees blotted them out. Rupert's body was warm and familiar beside hers. His arm around her shoulders felt comforting. His mindless gossip about mutual friends was pleasant. Meredith relaxed, letting her head fall back against his arm and her hand rest on his thigh.

He covered it with hand and began to toy with her fingers, light caresses designed to stir her desire.

Unfortunately, her body remained rigid, cool and uninterested in the sudden, warm pressure of his lips on the side of her neck.

"I've missed you, my dear. It's been too long." His breath against her face stank of cigars and whiskey.

Meredith turned toward his mouth and faced his kiss as if it were a punishment. She went through the motions of flirtation, laughingly accepting his compliments and kisses, his increasingly suggestive touches. His hand pressed between her thighs, seeking warmth through layers of dress and petticoat.

"You're too well-bundled. I think we need to go someplace more private." Rupert's eyes sparkled with lust and alcohol. He handed her his flask and she took a long drink.

"All right. Why not?"

Her body still felt like lead, not responding to him in any way, but maybe once out of her clothes she would begin to thaw. That was the way to erase Christopher from her mind. Rupert had always been a skilled lover. He would provide her satisfaction and make her forget Chris's inexperienced fumblings.

Soon she'd be her old, confident self, and the boy nothing more than the receding memory of a summertime fling.

ℰↃ

Meredith suggested they go to Rupert's house. She didn't want to entertain him in the familiarity of her own home. Or maybe it was the servants' censure she was avoiding, which was something she'd never considered or worried about before. Her staff was used to her guests spending the night. In fact, she thought they might rather enjoy their mistress's eccentricity which made her household a much more interesting place of employment than most.

But she knew the servants had liked Chris. With no words spoken, she'd felt the general warmth toward him. Cecile had been particularly eloquent in her disapproving silence after their return to London. Her cinching of Meredith's corset earlier that evening had been nothing short of torture.

Stopping at Rupert's town house was definitely preferable to bringing him home. Besides, that way she could leave whenever she wished.

By the time they entered the foyer of the Chadwick's once elegant home, now in shabby disrepair due to Rupert's gambling debts, Meredith could barely walk straight. She'd taken control of the flask and drunk deeply and, as she'd predicted, her body began to loosen and warm under the influence of alcohol and Rupert's hands.

She fell against him in the front hall, pushing his topcoat and jacket off his shoulders. He shrugged out of the heavy garments, letting them drop to the floor.

Her hands squeezed his biceps through his fine silk shirt. She pulled the tail of the shirt from his trousers and slipped a palm underneath. His stomach was a little paunchy from a life of nothing more strenuous than playing cards and drinking, but he was solid, warm, male, and most importantly, there.

Pushing away comparisons to Chris's body, the sound of his voice, the particular way he kissed her, Meredith focused on the man she was with. It was going to be all right. Rupert's hot, wet mouth covering hers was fine. His kiss sent a sweet ache through her breasts. Her nipples drew tight. Her pussy heated and clenched in response. Her body was reacting exactly as it should. If there was still a core of coldness within her, it was simply from the long carriage ride in the chilly night air.

Rupert's hands spread across her back, he kissed a trail down her jaw and neck and nuzzled at the swell of her breasts. He stood between her spread legs, and his erection pressed into her. Closing her eyes, she relaxed into the pleasure his mouth, hands and body gave.

When he pulled away, he was breathing hard. His eyes glowed in the candlelight that illuminated the foyer.

"I've missed this, all the good times we used to have. Remember the time we had sex with Highgate's mistress...what was her name? Pamela? That was quite a night!"

Meredith remembered. Unbridled passion, three bodies twining together in every possible combination, silky skin, rough stubble, cocks, breasts, pussies and hands, hands, hands touching and stroking everywhere. She licked her lips and squeezed her thighs together to ease her throbbing pussy.

Rupert brushed his thumb over her lower lip, his hungry eyes trained on her mouth.

"I have a pretty young housemaid, Ginny or Jenny, something like that. If I called her down from her bed, we could have another such entertaining evening. What do you think?"

The icicle inside Meredith spread tentacles of frost to her limbs. Her aching pussy went suddenly numb.

"Would young Ginny or Jenny have a choice in whether she wishes to participate?"

"Of course! I'd never take advantage of a servant."

"How young?"

"I'm not really sure. Her breasts are well-budded so she's past puberty at any rate. Fresh in from Devonshire. These country lasses blossom early, all that wholesome air and milk, I suppose." He laughed. "And her little cunny is so tight and hot you wouldn't believe..."

Meredith's fingers clenched, her nails digging into her palms. Naturally the girl would do whatever her master bid for fear of losing her place. No matter that he was jovial in his request. It was still a command as far as the girl was concerned.

"I think not, Rupert. Not tonight." She tucked her

spilling cleavage back into her bodice and smoothed down the front of her skirt. "As a matter of fact, I still feel rather queasy from earlier. I'm afraid I must bid you goodnight."

"No, Meredith! Rest in my bed a while. I'll give you something for your stomach and you'll feel better in a bit. The evening doesn't have to be a total loss."

"I'm sorry. I really need to leave." Meredith felt the need quite literally. She wanted to push him aside, bolt out the door and run all the way home.

"Now," she added firmly. "Will you call your driver for me, or must I walk?"

Rupert's mouth thinned to a straight line beneath the brush of his moustache. A frown furrowed his brow. "Very well."

He shrugged and offered a weak smile. "I guess, Jinny and I will have to make do with each other tonight."

Meredith stooped to pick up her cloak, which lay in a wine-red pool on the marble floor. Shivering, she pulled it around her shoulders and faced the man who'd once been her friend and occasional bed-partner.

"Rupert, don't. Let the girl sleep in peace tonight."

She walked back out into the cold, black night. Wind whistled down the empty street, driving dead leaves before it and cutting right through her cloak.

Meredith shook uncontrollably. She felt as desolate and fragile as the powder dry leaves that lodged against her foot. The heat of whiskey in her blood had evaporated. She thought she'd never be warm again.

Chapter Twelve

Chris walked the familiar paths of the Botanical Gardens for what might be the last time in a very long time...perhaps forever. He might choose not to return from his travels. If the specimens he gathered and documented were important enough and he could keep the grant money coming, he might not return to England for years.

He paused to examine the broad, flat leaves of a palm, then crouched to study a lichen growing on the trunk, noting the shape and color and identifying it automatically. Breathing deeply, he inhaled the loamy scent of the earth in which the tree's gnarled roots grew and thought about what it would be like to be rootless, free to travel to India or the Americas, from forest to swampland, jungle to desert, anywhere there was unique plant life.

When he'd shared the news of his appointment at the university and his impending departure to China for a year's study of medicinal plants, his father and mother had been shocked. Actually, that was putting it mildly. Father had roared like a lion and Mother had nearly fainted, although the latter was more a theatrical than an actual condition.

"What the hell is wrong with you, boy? Why can't we have a normal son, who'll act like a man and carry on the family name? Why in the world would you want to go to a heathen country, where you can catch some foreign disease, just to look at a bunch of...plants!" Father spat the last word like it was stuck to his tongue.

Chris didn't bother answering the rhetorical questions nor did he bring up his knowledge of his father conspiring with the countess. There was really no point. Nothing he could say would lessen his father's fury.

And nothing would assuage his own bitter sense of betrayal.

Instead, he'd turned and walked silently from the room. In that small, defiant act, a strength and calmness settled over him. He wondered if Father had already done his return favor for the countess, because the old man surely wouldn't consider their deal resolved to his satisfaction now. His son wasn't planning on fitting into society nor was he anywhere near close to choosing a wife and getting an heir.

As he had hundreds of times over the past few weeks, Chris wondered about the bill that had been so important to Meredith she'd been willing to sell her body to see it passed. He still felt a sharp stab of pain every time he thought of her.

Snubbing her at the dance hadn't satisfied him nearly as much as he'd expected. In fact, it had made him feel worse. His childish need to try to hurt her had dissipated the moment he'd turned his back on her. But when he'd looked for her, intending to go someplace private for a talk, she was leaving the ballroom with another man.

His heart had plummeted to his new, stylish boots, and he'd stood rooted to the spot as Hortense Simon prattled on about her new curricle. It was really over between them. Chris was no more to Meredith than any one of the numerous lovers she'd played with over the years. He was expendable, and she was finished with him.

The desire to crawl into bed and never emerge was nearly overwhelming, but he refused to give into it. Although a shroud of sadness wrapped around him like a dark cloud, he knew it couldn't last forever. Some day he would get over Meredith just as she'd told him he would. In time, memories of her silky hair trailing across his chest, her moist mouth, velvet-soft skin and wide, luminous eyes would fade. Maybe someday they'd be replaced by new memories of another woman, but if not, he'd be fine carrying on the work he enjoyed and seeing the exotic places he'd always dreamed about.

The day following the ball he'd gone to Cambridge to see the Dean of Science about prospects of employment at the university. He'd miraculously managed to bypass a teaching job and go straight to his fondest desire, the opportunity of study in China.

After speaking to his parents, Chris had gone to his room and packed. He'd moved to a hotel that very afternoon so he wouldn't have to suffer their tirades or wounded silences in the days preceding his departure.

Tonight, with only two days before he sailed, he'd been drawn back to the one place that had been a sanctuary to him in this city. The fact that it was the place where he'd first kissed Meredith was bound to haunt him, but he tried to push that particular memory out of his mind and concentrate on the burgeoning plant life that thrived on either side of the path.

Ceratozamia latifolia, Xanthoria parietina, Ficus carica, Muscari comosum—the names almost served to distract him from thoughts of light, rippling laughter and a soft, throaty voice, the caress of gentle hands and images of bound, naked beauty. Yet somehow he wasn't surprised when his feet led him toward the secluded spot in the jungle room where he'd first held Meredith in his arms.

He remembered sitting stiffly on that bench beside her and wondering if he was imagining her interest in him. He'd never drawn much female attention before and it seemed impossible such a sophisticated lady could be attracted to him. Of course, he'd been right. It was all an illusion or simply an amusing game to her. The once sweet memory of their first kiss became bitter. Perhaps it was best he face that place where they'd kissed and exorcise all thoughts of the Countess of Lies. She didn't matter now, he told himself. She was part of the past. He would put her behind him at last before setting sail into his future.

As he neared the path that led to the bench just off the main walking route, he stopped. The sound of a woman quietly weeping floated through the air from the other side of a scarlet mass of bougainvillea. His pulse sped up and the hair on his neck rose. No. It couldn't be her. The countess never cried. Not even when she'd talked about her foul, abusive husband or when Chris had unbound her from the bedposts and held her shaking body in his arms after that intense sexual encounter. It must be some other woman with a broken heart releasing her pain in what she imagined was the privacy of the grove.

He walked quietly around the edge of the flowering vines and looked toward the stone bench. All he could see was a woman's dove-gray skirt and a black shoe exposed by the raised hem. It couldn't be the countess, who always wore rich colors reminiscent of exotic jungle flowers. But another step around the tangle of vines at the exact moment she leaned forward, resting her elbows on her knees and her head in her hands, revealed that the woman on the bench was indeed Meredith.

Her shoulders shook and the heels of her hands were pressed into her eyes. She pulled her hands away long enough for Chris to see her face was blotched, puffy and stained with tears.

Her mouth opened to draw in a shaky breath when she noticed him standing there. Her pink-rimmed eyes widened, and on a soft breath she exhaled his name. "Chris."

His carefully constructed wall of indifference crumbled. The passion, fury and hopeless love that had been dammed behind it burst forth. He approached her, uncertain of whether he was going to grab her shoulders, shake her and yell into her face how much he hated her, or pull her into his arms and cover her with kisses. Trapped in an agony of indecision, he stopped several paces in front of her, hands clenched at his sides.

For a few beats of time, which felt like eternity, they stared at one another.

Her teary gray eyes were like rain clouds. Her distraught expression brought a surge of gladness. He wanted her to hurt as much as he did. But the thought was instantly followed by a desire to embrace and comfort her. He never wanted her to feel pain, but to protect her from it always. The conflicting feelings tumbled through him as he continued to remain frozen.

Finally he pushed a single word from his mouth. "Why?"

It was the key that unlocked a torrent of words. They spilled from her mouth like rain bursting from a cloud. "I'm sorry. I'm so sorry. I never meant to hurt you. The arrangement I made with your father was before I knew you. We agreed to trade favors. I told you I've had many affairs in my life, and I assumed this would be another diversion with no repercussions. I didn't know it would be you."

"And what if it had been some other naïve young man who came to care for you? That wouldn't matter?"

"Most men I've known are happy to have a no-strings-attached liaison. I didn't think..." She choked and swallowed and new tears trickled down her cheeks.

"No. You didn't think." He was amazed at how very cold his voice sounded when he felt such a hot turmoil of emotions. The desire to cuddle and caress her tears away fought against the wish to slap her, which warred with the need to fuck her until she wailed with pleasure.

"But I did warn you it was temporary," she reminded him, sniffing pitifully. She sounded like a penitent young girl rather than the controlled, sophisticated woman he'd first met.

"That's true. It was my fault. I convinced myself you only needed time to realize you were in love with me. I didn't know it was a farce from the very beginning."

She rubbed her eyes hard and rose from the bench. "I did a despicable thing and I'm sorry. Do you believe me?"

As incredible as it seemed, despite everything, he did believe her. Besides, she was crying before he arrived and had looked shocked to see him. These were genuine tears, not an act put on for his benefit.

Still he didn't say anything or move toward her. Inertia held him rooted in place.

"My agreement with your father wasn't the reason I wanted to end our relationship. I was afraid of being in love so I convinced myself I didn't believe in it. And I didn't want to marry any man and put myself under his control. Not after what I went through the first time." Her sorrowful eyes held him fast. Her hands were held open beseechingly as she took a step toward him.

"I can understand that," Chris conceded quietly. "But tell me, what exactly was your deal with my father?"

Her pink cheeks reddened further. "I was to help you emerge from your shell and become...more confident around women. In return, your father promised to support the millworkers' bill."

"How did that benefit you?" His arms folded across his chest as though protecting his heart and blocking her advances.

"The bill is concerned with better working conditions. I've already increased wages and improved safety in the mill I own, but I can't compete if the rest of the owners don't do the same. The expense was slowly putting me out of business. I needed that bill to pass—for the laborers' safety, but also for my financial success."

Her action was hardly noble, yet Chris couldn't help but be pleased she'd at least used him, in a twisted way, for a good cause.

"I guess that's how things work in politics. People are literally fucked in order for someone else to accomplish an agenda."

His acid tone made her flinch, and her open hands dropped to her sides.

"You have a right to be bitter. I never thought of your feelings, just what I needed. But I want you to know that although it may have begun as a business arrangement, it became more than that. You were right. I do have feelings for you—powerful feelings that won't go away. I wish I didn't, but there it is. I think I'm in l-love with you." She stammered the word and finished on a broken sob.

She looked so miserable and mortified by her admission that Chris nearly smiled.

Rubbing her hands over her eyes, she cleared them of

tears and focused on him again. "Can you forgive me? Is it too late?"

"I'm not bitter," he lied, glancing up to where the leaves of the *Ceratozamia kuesteriana* touched the ceiling overhead. "Because of you, I gained the courage to pursue what I want. I'm leaving for China on a field expedition in a few days."

"Leaving?"

His gaze swept down the length of the tree and back to her face. Beneath the pink blotches, her face was pale.

"I have to do this. I have to take control of my life and follow my dream."

"I know. Of course you should go. You must." Her lips and chin trembled and her eyes glistened. "I only want you to be happy, Christopher."

A silent moment ticked by while he thought about all she had revealed, all he could easily hate her for, and all he was willing to forgive. Her penitent words and tear-streaked face went a long way toward softening his resolve to put her and every memory of her behind him.

Finally he allowed a small smile to curve his lips. "Do you know what would make me happy? If you took the journey with me. You're a very wealthy woman. I'm sure you could afford the passage."

Her wet-lashed eyes widened. "To China...with you?"

"Didn't you tell me you always wanted to travel? That hearing about exotic locations was the one part of your husband's homecoming you actually enjoyed?"

She moved toward him. "You forgive me and want me back?"

Chris broke his defensive stance, dropping his arms to his sides. "Do you even need to ask? I told you before I love you. I didn't say it lightly."

He held his arms open and she rushed into them, throwing her arms around his neck and pressing against him. He held her soft, scented body close, burrowed his nose into the side of her neck and breathed her in. It was like a miracle. He'd convinced himself he'd never have this again, that the gaping hole torn in his heart would be permanent, but here she was, filling his arms and his heart once more.

Her body trembled and after a moment, she pulled away to look into his face. Tears streamed down her face, but laughter competed with her sobs. "I'm a mess. I haven't been able to stop crying for days."

"Making up for lost years." He wiped her cheek, then leaned to cover her mouth with his, tasting salty tears. Her lips parted at the pressure of his mouth, permitting his tongue inside. Her tongue coiled around his like the tendril of a vine seeking a place to hold onto.

He kissed her until he was dizzy from lack of breath before pulling away. "So... Will you go with me?"

Her eyes moved back and forth, scanning his. "I will."

"Your business affairs won't suffer if you take an extended leave?" He caressed the small of her back through the fabric of her dress. Why had he asked such a foolish question? Did he want to give her an opportunity to back out?

Meredith shook her head. "I have a manager I trust. Not as much as I trust myself, of course, but he'll maintain things. I can book my passage today. And if there's no room left on the ship, I'll stow away."

"Mm, a stowaway in my cabin. How very romantic." He smiled and rested his forehead against hers. "Of course, I'll request sexual favors in order to keep your secret."

"I'll be at your command." Her arms were around his waist now and her hands gliding up his back underneath his jacket. "Whatever you want to do with me, I'll have to submit."

Although they were only teasing, his cock leaped at the word "submit". He pressed his erection against her, seeking some relief through layers of fabric. Tilting his head, he found her lips again and nuzzled lightly. He kissed the corners, sucked her full lower lip into his mouth, then let it go before settling his mouth firmly over hers and taking control. Kissing her hard and deep, he claimed her as his own. He wouldn't lie to himself and say he had no residual anger about the game she'd played with his life, but it seemed a minor thing compared to the joy of having Meredith back in his arms again.

They kissed frantically, touching each other all over, loosening hooks and buttons so their fingers could reach flesh underneath. There were far too many clothes separating them, but Chris didn't want to break apart from her long enough to get a carriage and drive to a different location. He had to have her here and now, to make a covenant with their bodies, and to make up for the past, torturous weeks without her.

The sound of children's voices and a woman answering them came from around the bend. Chris broke off the kiss and searched for a more private place. "Here." He took her hand and pulled her off the path, behind the *Cycad* palms and an outcropping of rock over which water tumbled into a small pool. He led her to a shadowy space between rock and smooth tree trunks. More of the thick leaves and lush flowers of bougainvillea vines shielded the spot. No one could see them in this narrow alcove, unless they, too, strayed from the path.

"Look, Nanny! Fishes!" a childish voice piped.

Chris clutched Meredith close and smiled at her. Their breath brushed one another's faces as their chests rose and fell in sync. They huddled in their shelter and listened to the exclamations of several children feeding the orange and black Koi that circled the pool on the far side of the rock.

He lowered his mouth and kissed her while reaching for the plump fullness of her breasts hidden behind her bodice. The soft mounds rested in the cups of her corset, and he snaked his hand into the neckline of her gown to feel them yield beneath his palm and fingers. A powerful tide of lust swelled his cock.

He pulled his mouth from hers and bent to press a kiss to her chest. He slicked his tongue over her collarbones and the flat plane that led to the round curves of her cleavage. Cupping one breast, he pushed it up from below. It bobbed toward freedom and his waiting mouth. He took the red nipple between his lips, drawing on it with hard sucks.

Meredith gasped and thrust her chest toward his face. Her fingers gripped his skull, holding him to her.

Doing scandalous things in a public place with the possibility of discovery heightened every sensation. Chris's flesh tingled all over. He wanted to tear off his clothes and hers so they could fuck as freely as Adam and Eve in the Garden—except with passers-by only a few yards away. The voices of the children and their nanny had moved on, but newcomers were approaching.

Chris finished sucking one nipple to a pebbled point and turned his attention to the other. He glanced at Meredith's flushed face. Her eyes were closed and she panted softly. A little, animalistic whine escaped her throat, and she rolled her head against the rough rock against which he had pushed her. "More!" she moaned quietly. "Fuck me!"

His balls drew tight at the sound of her begging and his cock strained against his breeches. He reached for the hem of her skirt and petticoat and pulled it above her waist, tucking the folds of fabric into the front of her bodice to keep them out of the way. His hand slipped into her drawers against the warmth of her taut stomach and through the curls that guarded her sex like a fluffy hedge. He exhaled a low groan when his fingers finally encountered her plump labia and the dripping wet opening of her sex and pushed inside.

"Ah!" Meredith's sharp gasp twisted his insides and tightened the tension another notch. He felt he'd snap like an over-tuned guitar string if he didn't shove his cock inside her within the next few seconds. Her lessons about breath control were forgotten. He didn't care about prolonged pleasure and only wanted to bury himself balls deep in her body, which was yearning toward his probing fingers.

After thrusting in and out a few times, he pulled his hand free and fumbled with the fly of his breeches. Her hands joined his, helping him release his aching cock. She grasped it and squeezed tight around the base. With her other fist she stroked all the way up and rubbed her thumb over the weeping slit at the crown. Her glittering eyes met his. "Shall I suck it?" she whispered.

He shook his head and pushed her back against the rock again. "I need to be inside you. Right. Now!" He emphasized the words through gritted teeth, as he pushed her hands away from his cock. He jerked her drawers lower.

Her skirts began to slip, and Meredith hoisted them up out of the way. As he cupped his hands under the curve of her bottom and lifted her, she wrapped her thighs around his waist. Her ankles were trapped together because of her dangling undergarment binding them together, but she was able to grip his waist between her knees. His cock nudged blindly at her entrance.

Chris reached between them and guided her onto his erect staff. The warm humidity surrounding them in the room of glass and steel was nothing compared to the steamy tropical rainforest inside her body. She enveloped him, her inner muscles drawing him deeper, inch-by-inch, until he hit her very womb.

"Ahh, Chrisss!" His name came out a loud, sibilant hiss, which blended with the steady rush of water on the other side of the rock. Her hands gripped his shoulders. She writhed against the boulder behind her and ground her hips into his.

He grunted as he pulled out and thrust in again, gravity pulling her down onto him as he drove up inside her hard and fast. Sweat coated his skin beneath his vest, shirt and undershirt. It trickled down his chest, back and arms. Droplets slipped down the length of his legs under heavy wool trousers. Moisture pooled between their thrusting bodies. Their groins slapped together wetly. A light breeze tickled his naked ass and he wished their foolish clothes would disappear altogether, leaving them the way Nature intended.

Her skirts were bunched between them. God, he wanted them out of the way. He wanted to see her totally nude here in this private-public spot, to see pale, delicate limbs sprawled against rough granite. His cock felt like stone as he pulled out and slid in with another grunt.

Harder, deeper, he speared her. The primitive need to claim her as his mate, to possess her and drive off all other males filled him. The bit of him that was still a sane, educated man with forward views on a woman's place in society was intrigued by the phenomenon. As a scholar, he realized he was experiencing a primal urge beyond his control. The animal part of his brain was uppermost now.

He'd once feared and fought against that devolution of intellect into animal desire, but now embraced it. And when his countess sweetly moaned, "Harder!" he was more than happy to oblige her.

The voices from the path seemed dim and unimportant. Only the pair of them here, locked in this ancient embrace, mattered. His groans grew louder as the ecstasy centered in his groin strengthened. His balls drew up tight while his cock swelled and filled her tight channel even more. And then it exploded in a blossoming of pure rapture.

He pushed up even tighter against her, crushing her between his body and stone. His fingers dug into her tender thighs and his forehead rested on her shoulder as he released in rhythmic pulses deep inside her. Ragged gasps tore in and out of his chest. His lips pressed against the soft flesh just above her collarbone and he sucked it into his mouth, tasting her salty skin, breathing her rose perfume. *Love. My love.* His mind murmured what his lips would not. Not so soon. He was too unsure of her reaction. He didn't want to frighten her away. *Love you. Want you with me always.*

Her hands combed through his hair and clutched the back of his head and neck, holding him to her. He felt her light kiss against the side of his neck, and she murmured something into his skin. Perhaps she was saying what he was thinking, but her words weren't loud enough to hear.

After several moments, Chris straightened and let Meredith slide down his body to stand on her own. He tucked his cock in his breeches and fastened them, then helped her with her clothes, crouching to straighten the hem of her skirt while she pushed her breasts back into the neckline of her bodice.

"Do I look all right?" she whispered. Her hair was as wild as though she'd just risen from bed. Half of it tumbled from its pins while the rest remained firmly in place.

He rose and leaned to kiss her lips. "You look perfect." His hands threaded through the tangled mane of hair and held her head as he kissed her deeply. "Just perfect to me."

Chapter Thirteen

Meredith stood on the hillside with a carpet of blue at her feet. It was just as Chris had described it to her—a huge meadow of gentian flowers cupped in a fold of the mountains. Between the cerulean on the ground and the glorious azure sky overhead, she felt she was in the center of a vast, blue heaven. A bracing breeze blew steadily against her, pulling strands of hair from the single braid she'd plaited and whipping them around her face. Even with her heavy coat, mittens, scarf wrapped around her neck and a hood pulled over her head, she was cold. Her nose and cheeks were numb from the chill wind, but the amazing sight of the flowery field was worth a little discomfort.

Christopher closed his sample case and came to stand beside her. He wrapped an arm around her waist and hugged her. Together they gazed at the scenic beauty of the wilderness. "What do you think? Worth the trip?"

She turned to him and smiled through chattering teeth. "It's not the first place that would've come to mind on my list of countries to visit, but I'm very glad to be here." *To be anywhere with you.* She'd almost literally followed him to the ends of the earth. The journey to the Orient had been long and arduous. She'd been seasick on the voyage, then jolted unmercifully in various horse-drawn conveyances on rough, rocky roads. The food and water had made her ill, too, and at times she wished she'd never left England.

But when all those physical difficulties resolved, she began to enjoy the journey. The sights, sounds and smells of a foreign land were all around her. China was thrilling, mystifying, beautiful and horrible in its rich culture and unrelenting poverty. Holding Chris's hand as they toured ancient temples, climbed mountain paths or strolled in exotic marketplaces was wonderful. Lying in his arms at night was the best part of the trip. They made love in hotel rooms and huts, in the luxury of a bed or on the rocky floor of a ravine. They coupled in every way imaginable, and Meredith never felt the jaded ennui she'd come to expect after months spent with a lover. Every time with Chris was like a new beginning.

He grabbed her mittened hand and gave it a tug. "Come. Let's find some shelter. This wind is bitter."

She was glad he'd said it first. She hated to complain.

Following the slight trampled path they'd made through the hardy wildflowers, they walked uphill until they came to a rocky outcropping that shielded them from the cutting breeze while still affording a vista of the valley and mountains beyond.

Meredith tossed back her hood and removed her mittens. She pulled the scarf away from her mouth and took the flask Chris offered her. A molten gold trickle of brandy burned down her throat and settled in her belly, suffusing her with a warm glow.

"Better?" Chris had removed his hat, and his hair stood up in a static-filled thicket. His cheeks glowed and his eyes were as bright a blue as the gentians.

She laughed and smoothed her hand through his hair. "My crazy professor. You love being here, don't you? You thrive on it."

"On being with you." His smile made her even warmer than the brandy. "Don't you know it doesn't matter to me whether I'm on an expedition or working in your conservatory? I just want to be with you."

"Then perhaps our next journey could be someplace more tropical." She unfastened the top button of her coat. "Someplace where we can wear fewer clothes."

Chris glanced at the tall rock walls sheltering them. "We're fairly protected here. I think we can shed a few layers and still keep warm." His merry eyes and seductive smile raised her temperature, and suddenly she was glad to shed her coat.

With lightning speed and frantic fingers, they stripped down to their underwear. Chris made a soft nest of the discarded coats and dragged Meredith down to lie on it beside him. He pulled her close against his warm body, throwing a casual leg over hers and wrapping his arms tight around her. "It's not so bad." His breath was a silvery puff in the air. "Although I do miss your big, soft bed."

She pressed her chilled nose into the hollow of his throat, breathing him in while she warmed it. He smelled like fresh air with a tang of wood smoke from the campfire earlier. A light flick of her tongue against his skin added the trace of sweat and man-flesh to her sensual feast. Sometimes she simply wanted to devour him or to wrap herself up in his body so completely that they became one.

His hands splayed on her back, rubbing up and down, warming her, then slipping below her waist to gently knead her bottom. He slipped a hand between her legs and fingered her pussy through the thin material. Her slit opened and yearned toward his touch, wetting her drawers with moisture. She squirmed against him and thrust herself back against his teasing fingers.

It occurred to her that they'd engaged in intercourse for weeks now on an almost daily basis—weeks without the interruption of her monthly cycle. Doctors had assured her long ago she was infertile, but recently she'd begun to wonder if they'd been wrong. It was difficult to believe years of sexual activity with no protection other than ensuring her partners weren't syphilis carriers hadn't resulted in an accidental pregnancy at some point. But now it seemed possible she wasn't barren and may have, in fact, conceived. Since she'd resigned herself to never having children, the idea was too incredible to examine closely, or to share with Chris. Not until she was certain there was news to share.

How would he feel about such a thing? Would he prefer to remain childless, both of them free to travel the world? Would he demand marriage if there was a child to consider? She worried about what his reaction might be if the impossible became fact.

"What's wrong?" He stopped toying with her bottom and pulled back from her, peering into her eyes.

"Nothing." How did he know? He seemed to have an unerring instinct where she was concerned.

"There's something," he insisted. "Today. Yesterday. The last couple of days something has been on your mind." His brow was furrowed and his eyes serious. "Are you tired of traveling? Do you want to go home?"

"No. That's not it."

"Ah. Then there is something." He cupped her face and traced his thumb along her jaw.

He was too clever by far and too in tune with her emotions. It was rather frightening to have someone that aware of the subtle nuances of her voice and demeanor.

She forced a laugh. "Nothing. Really."

But he kept gazing into her eyes and rubbing her cheek. "Tell me."

"I simply realized I...haven't had my monthly cycle as I should have by now."

His eyes widened. "How long?"

She paused and recalled the days and nights with him. "Since before I met you. I never counted the days or even thought about it until recently. My cycle has never been regular and it's not supposed to be possible for me to be..." She trailed off, unable to voice the word "pregnant".

His thumb stilled on her face, but his hand remained there, cradling her jaw. She scanned his eyes for a reaction and for a moment they remained blank. No, not blank, thoughtful. She didn't realize she'd caught her breath until a slow smile curved his lips and she released it.

Chris looked deeply into her eyes. "This is...unexpected. How would you feel if it were true?"

"I don't know. I've only begun to wonder and didn't want to tell you until I was sure. There may be no cause for alarm."

"I wouldn't be alarmed," he assured her. "All right. Perhaps a little frightened, but no more than would be normal for any expectant father."

Father. That would make her a mother. And the three of them would be a family. Such an odd thought.

"I'm afraid," she blurted. "Afraid it might be true and afraid it might not be. I can't imagine myself a mother. I was only just getting used to the idea of you and me together and the idea of having a child terrifies me and thrills me. Everything would change."

"Yes." He shifted beside her, moving up on the makeshift pallet and drawing her head down onto his chest. He squeezed her tight and shared his body heat with her. "Life changes suddenly sometimes."

"I suppose you'd want to marry." She listened to his heartbeat thumping behind his hard breastbone. "To save the child being called a bastard."

"Are you proposing to me?" His warm chuckle vibrated her ear. "Countess, you know where I stand on the subject. You're the one with doubts."

She thought about her fear of giving up her freedom once more, of putting herself in the vulnerable position of trusting a man and losing her hard-earned assets when she took his name. The idea of Christopher abusing her trust or her body was ludicrous, yet she hesitated.

"You know, just because we marry doesn't mean we can't circumvent the law," he said. "We could draw up a legal document in which you'd retain the rights to all your properties and possessions. I wouldn't ever want you to feel you'd given up your right to be your own person. Would that make you more amenable to the idea of marriage?"

"Marriage." She sighed. "I knew you'd suggest that."

"And why not? Our child, should we have one, deserves to have a proper home."

She nearly smiled when he said "our child", but it wouldn't do to appear too ready to capitulate. "I suppose," she answered.

He kissed the top of her head and his hand began to wander again, squeezing a handful of her buttock lightly. "Think about it. There's no reason you can't have both your freedom and a family, too."

"And if I'm not with child?" She lifted her head and propped her arms on his chest so she could see him.

Chris paused before answering. "You know how I feel about that, too. I'd love to enter into a legally binding

191

contract with you that would label us 'husband' and 'wife', but if you never choose to do that it doesn't change what we have together." He looked intently into her eyes. "There's a phenomenon in nature called a symbiotic relationship. Certain animals and plants depend upon one another for their very existence. I believe that whether we call it marriage or not, you and I exist in such a relationship." He lifted his head and leaned toward her, seeking a kiss. His voice lowered to a husky whisper as he added, "I know I couldn't exist without you."

He was so very sweet sometimes it made her ache all over. She inclined her head and kissed his cool lips. Her own were just as cold, but together they grew warm...and then hot. Her tongue swept into his mouth and thrust against his, while he dragged her on top of him, pulling her coat over her to keep her naked backside warm.

Thoughts of her possible pregnancy were momentarily pushed aside as Meredith let lust overwhelm her. She moved on him, rubbing her body against his as though they were two pieces of wood that might strike enough sparks to light a fire. The slow, smooth slide of skin on skin soon had a nice blaze glowing in her sex.

She pulled away from kissing him long enough to gasp, "You were right. It's actually warmer without clothes on."

"I'm usually right. You should listen to me often." He nipped her earlobe to punctuate his words.

Her clit tightened as she slid over him again, her pussy gliding the length of his shaft like a long, wet kiss.

She was already primed for him. It took very little, sometimes merely the sound of his voice, a look or a smile, to make her sex grow hard and wet.

Her nipples were taut and sensitive. When they brushed against the smooth muscles of his chest and the fine down that covered it, they felt like they'd burst from the exquisite tension of that slight touch.

His hands slid down her back and clutched her ass, once more kneading the firm flesh, then pulling her cheeks apart and sliding a finger down the groove between them. The coat thrown over her back didn't cover her completely and her bottom was bare to the chill breeze. The caress of cool air on her genitals and Chris's stroking finger around the rim of her anus had her pussy open and dripping. She couldn't take any more stimulation and needed him inside her immediately.

Meredith pushed up on one arm and reached between them to guide his cock to her waiting slit. She positioned him just at the entrance, then sat up straight, heedless of the coat slipping off and leaving her body naked to the cold. She accepted him into her, settling slowly on top of him to make the experience last. Looking down, she watched her pussy swallow his cock until not an inch was left.

She looked from their joined bodies to Chris's face. His eyes, too, were riveted on the place of union. He glanced up at her and grinned. "A perfect fit. I think we're meant to be together."

Bracing her hands against his chest, she rose up on

her knees, revealing his penis again, then enveloped him once more. Up and down she rode, squeezing her inner muscles around his girth to enhance the sensation. He groaned and thrust his hips, spearing her deeply each time she bore down on him.

Meredith continued to watch his face through eyes half-closed in pleasure. She rocked a little from side to side, then back and forth, experimenting with different positions and variations in rhythm before settling into a steady bounce. She rose and fell on top of him, heat flushing her skin, sweat rising on her body and drying in the cool air.

He grasped her breasts, rolling and pulling the nipples, then took hold of her upper arms and pulled her down to him. Lifting his head, he sucked a nipple into his mouth. The tugging sensation at her tit and the wonderfully filled feeling in her quim came together, building faster and faster to an explosive climax. She cried out at the force of it and rammed herself on his erect cock with such force that he grunted at the impact.

Inspired by the strength of her release, Chris thrust into her once more and let out a hoarse animalistic cry of his own. His head was rolled back, exposing his neck. His eyes were closed, the lashes laying in two beautiful crescents against his cheeks. She was struck by the beauty of his face transported by bliss.

She collapsed on top of him, sinking back into the warmth of his body as her breathing slowly returned to normal.

"I love you," she confided to his neck.

"I love you, too," he gasped, still winded from his vigorous thrusting. "And whether we have a child or not, whether we marry or not, nothing changes that."

The countess smiled and smoothed a hand over his firm, muscled chest, such a strong, manly chest for a botanist to have. She wondered how the conservatory was doing back at home. Was her gardener taking good care of the plants and were they thriving? Some day she and Chris would sit together there with a humid jungle of plants surrounding them and remember how barren and dry it used to be.

In her illogical heart, she felt that love and not manure-enriched soil had brought that greenhouse back to life, the love that Chris had given her with no expectation of returned feelings. Because he asked for nothing, she wanted to give him everything—an abundance of joy, a wealth of pleasure and every part of her that she had to share. She hoped she was pregnant. She'd like to give him a child, too.

Her heart was as open and vulnerable as a newly bloomed flower, but Meredith felt no need to shield it. She knew the fragile petals were safe in her lover's care.

About the Author

To learn more about Bonnie Dee, please visit http://bonniedee.com. Send an email to Bonnie Dee at bondav40@yahoo.com or join her Yahoo! group to join in the fun with other readers as well as Bonnie Dee. http://groups.yahoo.com/group/bonniedee/

The camera took one last photo, one last still frame of a woman in the throes of abandon. And then it was silent, all its frames exposed, all of her secrets contained within one deceptively small, simple black box.

Captured

© 2007 Anna J. Evans

The year is 1897, and twenty-three-year-old Lillian Thomas possesses one of the first Kodak cameras. Despite Boston society's belief that women should be seen and not heard—and certainly never photographed in the nude—she is determined to proceed with a series of erotic self-portraits. Portraits that she hopes will lure the object of her darkest fantasies to her bed, and scandal to her name.

Alexander Darian can scarcely believe the girl he once knew has become a woman capable of such abandon. He knows the instant he lays eyes on the photographs of Lillian that he must have her, in every wicked way he imagines. No matter that her father has done his best to ruin Alexander, or that memories of their childhood romance have haunted him for longer than he cares to admit.

But passion isn't as easily manipulated as either lover assumes, and soon they begin to wonder—who is casting the net of seduction and who will find themselves captured?

Available now in ebook and print from Samhain Publishing.

Enjoy the following excerpt Captured...

"Let the sheet slide off your other shoulder, expose the other breast now." Alexander's voice was muffled by the camera he stood behind, but Lillian had no trouble hearing his directive. She did, however, have a great deal of trouble resisting the urge to tell the bastard exactly what he could do with his overbearing attitude.

"Of course." Her voice was remarkably calm, considering the mix of rage and maddening desire that thrummed through her body as she obeyed his command.

"Not so much. Try to *tease*, not simply bare yourself." Alexander sighed, but snapped a picture all the same. "We're looking to seduce the viewer, Lillian, not merely give him a refresher course on the female anatomy."

She wanted to kill him. No, on second thought, she wanted to lay him naked on a hill of fire ants, let them sting his flesh for hours, and *then* kill him. Instead she forced a seductive smile.

"*He* might also be a *she*, Zander. We women do enjoy erotic photographs, as well." Lillian shifted slightly on the settee and tried to think sensual thoughts rather than homicidal ones. She rearranged the sheet until only the barest hint of each nipple was showing and her long braid hung down over one shoulder, nearly covering the aureole of her left breast.

"Better." He said the words begrudgingly and turned to rearrange several of the dozen electric lamps.

Amazingly they hadn't blown a fuse as yet, but it was only a matter of time. Zander had a specially made light as large as a street lamp running, as well as the smaller lamps. They were surely only minutes from an overload.

Then they would be sitting in darkness together, alone in the business district after all the other shopkeepers had run home. There would be no one to hear the man scream when she pounced upon him like a wild animal and—

And what?

She'd brought this on herself by pretending she wanted something other than her true desire. How could she fault Zander for giving her exactly what she'd asked for? Deception was most assuredly a sin that cut both ways.

"Focus, Lillian. If you want to have a sufficient portfolio to send to Paris by the end of the month, you can't drift away each time I stop to rearrange the lights."

Or maybe she *could* fault him, the bastard. He'd kissed her on the beach, touched her intimately and given the clear impression that they would be doing more tonight than merely playing photographer and subject. Damn it, the man had even mentioned something about "lessons", bringing to mind all those deliciously naughty tales of schoolgirls turned over their tutor's knee.

She'd moved heaven and earth to sneak out of the house and down to his studio tonight, not to mention spent a good chunk of pocket money bribing the scullery maid. He would do more than take her picture tonight.

Her plan to make the man wait had been out the window hours ago. She *would* lose her virginity tonight, and Zander would be the man to permanently rid her of the last of her innocence.

"I'm sorry, Zander," Lillian said, an idea sparking in her fertile imagination. "Perhaps I'm having trouble because I don't know what I *should* be thinking about."

"What do you mean?"

"I mean, I've never been with a man in that way. How would I know how to go about seducing him with my eyes, or anything else for that matter?" Lillian arranged her face in her most innocent expression, even as one hand idly fingered the edge of the sheet near her tightened nipple.

Feeling his eyes on her, knowing she was nude for the first time in front of a man—this man—had kept her in a state of dizzying arousal for hours. It was likely near midnight, and her muscles ached from posing for him, but her wicked lust only grew more vicious. She desperately needed relief, and was determined that he would be the one to give it to her.

"I think you're doing a fairly good job." A smile quirked at the edge of his lips, but his eyes were dark and humorless as he snapped another picture.

"I am? Are you speaking as a man, or as a photographer?" Lillian held his gaze, nearly losing the ability to draw breath as those brown eyes seemed to stare straight through her, past the boundaries of her skin to the secrets of her very soul.

"Very well, Lillian." His voice was frighteningly soft as

he fetched the lens cap for his camera and slipped it into place. "I was going to wait until I felt we'd taken at least a dozen appropriate photographs, but if you are so eager to advance to the payment portion of the evening, I'm willing to oblige."

"Payment?" What in the world was he up to? Surely he didn't mean to blackmail her for money? The Zander she had known would never do such a thing, and this older, harder version of that boy had no need for money from the look of his home and studio. Perhaps he'd merely forgotten that she couldn't afford to pay him. "But I told you, Zander, I don't have—"

"Lesson number one. Nothing in the world is given freely, Lillian. This is something you must learn before you strike out alone. There are many out there who would lure you in with promises of friendship, only to pull out a marker later and demand all that you own. Never sign anything, never take a loan of money or service without consulting a lawyer or trusted advisor first." As he walked toward her, he slowly slipped off his coat and then moved his fingers to the buttons on the vest beneath.

Tess Starling is willing to risk everything—and offer anything—to avenge her father's death.

Carnal Deceptions
© 2007 Scottie Barrett

Upon leaving her father's gravesite, Tess spies creditors confiscating the finery of her first London Season. But her gowns will do little to satisfy her father's debts. Fleet Prison awaits her. Tess dons a homely disguise, cloaking herself in mourning weeds. She is determined to evade the authorities until she brings to justice the swindler who ruined her father. Resolute in her quest, she will transform anew, reinventing herself as a temptress to seduce the villain. She only wants for hands-on training, but the man who volunteers proves too much of a distraction. Everything about Tallon Hawkes, the Earl of Marcliffe, fascinates, including the battle scars marking his body. A motivated pupil, Tess yields eagerly to his sexual demands.

Long before he discovers the sensuous female beneath the layers of black crepe...long before he discovers the brilliant copper-colored tresses hidden by the ratty wig...long before he tastes the sweetness of her skin, Tallon Hawkes' heart has been hooked. Tallon plays along with Tess's scheme, but he is distrustful and jealous of her obsession with their shared enemy. Tallon is determined to bring her dangerous game to an end.

Available now in ebook and print from Samhain Publishing.

Enjoy the following excerpt from Carnal Deceptions...

The next morning, Tess woke to find herself tangled in her blankets. She'd been dreaming of satin and silk and erotic couplings. The explicit pictures that Miss Midwinter had shown her were branded on her brain. A woman bound with ropes, lifting her bottom in offering as she waited for the man to plunge into her. A woman servicing three men at once. Miss Midwinter had added her own narrative, describing the sexual acts depicted so graphically Tess had been forced to open the window to the chill morning air to cool her cheeks. All her lessons lacked were practice. Her dreams had revealed a deep hunger for that real experience. Unfortunately, in every dream Lord Marcliffe was the man she explored with her mouth and hands and body. She'd slid satin over the smooth skin of his chest until it snagged on the rough scars of his shoulder. More shockingly, she'd followed the trail of the fabric with her open mouth, her tongue tracing every ridge.

Frustrated, she threw her bedclothes aside. She stepped naked out of bed and bathed herself at the washstand. After patting herself dry, she opened the wardrobe and peered into a dark and empty hole. Not even her chemise hung there. She searched the floor, shook out the bedclothes, got on her knees to peer under the bed and found nothing, not a stitch. Even the flannel gown she'd thrown off in the night was gone. She wrapped herself in a blanket. Opening the door a crack, she called for help. No one answered. Her pleas seemed to echo off the walls.

Tess stepped into the hallway and raced down the stairs. There was a queer emptiness to the house. She shivered as her bare feet touched the cold tile floor of the entrance hall. With the heavy blanket dragging behind her, she entered the dining room. No weak tea or burnt toast awaited her. She pushed open the kitchen door expecting to see Mrs. Smith's smiling face, only to find another vacant room. Afraid now, she hurried up the stairs to Lady Stadwell's bedchamber. The door was ajar. She found the wardrobe empty as well as the bureau drawers.

She'd been deserted. She could not go into the yard naked, but she was certain what she would find there. No gardeners, no grooms, and the stable cleared of all horses.

Without question, she knew exactly who had executed this plan, who'd evacuated the house right under her nose. Trembling with fury, she returned to her chamber. Why not take advantage and luxuriate in bed for once? First she fluffed the pillow but then decided to give it a good pounding, until feathers burst from its seams. She settled back on the now flattened pillow, but finding rest in her agitated state proved impossible. With a scream of vexation, she kicked the covers to the floor then with a muttered oath stooped to retrieve the blanket. She had yet to explore Mrs. Smith's room. Determined to thwart the fiendish earl, Tess lit a candle and ascended the servants' stairs. The flame fluttered eerily in the narrow hallway. Muttering a plea for fortune to turn in her favor, she entered the low-ceilinged room. The doors on the small wardrobe were agape, and the barren interior that greeted her seemed a purposeful taunt. Not even a blasted apron remained.

Sparked by another idea, she raced downstairs to see if the mudroom that adjoined the kitchen held at least a rain cloak. The hooks were empty. The bastard had been ruthlessly thorough. If he wanted rid of her so badly, why hadn't he left her some clothing? Clearly, he wished to see her completely humiliated.

She stomped through the empty house. In the parlor, she clutched at the faded damask drapery, thinking to yank the curtains from the wall, but the curtain rod was too heavy and well-seated. She would have to take scissors to the fabric. It was an inspiration with little chance of success. Her skills as a seamstress were negligible. Besides, it would take her forever to create a garment. She glanced out the window at the stables. Though the house was somewhat isolated, certain angles of the yard could be spied from the road, and Tess did not have the courage to go outside mantled only in a blanket. When night fell, she'd fetch the ladder from the barn. She would explore the attic for moth-eaten garments. Surely there had to be remnants of other generations stored. Unable to occupy her mind with reading or anything remotely productive, she curled up on the settee to wait for dusk.

The sky was just starting to gray, the gloomy veil of night dropping, when the front door slammed. Tess flew off the settee and raced into the entrance hall, her bare feet skidding on the slick marble, to find the devil himself, with the two huge mastiffs at his heels. He gave her a placid smile as he pulled off his leather gloves. What was he up to? She didn't trust a hair on his black head.

"W-What is going on? Where is everyone?" she stammered, completely flustered by the idea of being alone with him.

"They left early, just before the sun. I had the cook accompany Lady Stadwell in the carriage so that people would think you'd left with her."

She eyed him suspiciously. "Why would you do that?" Her voice rose to a hysterical pitch and he immediately pressed his fingers to his temples.

Though he appeared stone cold sober, he was suffering the aftereffects of a week of imbibing. His skin was paler than usual and in stark contrast to his black hair. "Because people talk. And since we are just beginning this venture, I felt there was no need to stir up rumors."

Tess pulled the wool blanket tighter, scratching her bare skin. She had never felt so vulnerable. She blinked up in confusion at the most intimidating man she'd ever known. She was at his mercy. Lady Stadwell had abandoned her.

"Is there some reason—" With effort, she squelched the urge to rain curses down on him "—why I have nothing to wear?" Her voice vibrated with fury.

He shrugged. "The dressmaker will have some of your

wardrobe completed by the week's end. In the meantime, you won't need any clothing."

"I suppose I'm to lock myself in my room naked until she arrives?"

"No, I expect you to stay in *my* room naked for the week."

She couldn't have understood him correctly. "Pardon?"

"If I'm to hire you for my aunt's dubious scheme, I'd like to see just how capable you are."

"Exactly what does that mean?"

"I intend to fuck you, Miss Calloway."

Lord Marcliffe was studying her a little too carefully. She suspected he was expecting she'd lose her nerve. He casually combed back his windblown hair with his fingers. How on earth could someone be that handsome and that cruel? "I detest you!"

GREAT
cheap
fun

Discover eBooks!

THE FASTEST WAY TO GET THE HOTTEST NAMES

Get your favorite authors on your favorite reader, long before they're
out in print! Ebooks from Samhain go wherever you go, and work with
whatever you carry—Palm, PDF, Mobi, and more.

Printed in the United States
143031LV00001B/104/P

9 781605 041582